ONCE A LONG TIME AGO

MIKE SMITH

Dedication

To Carrie my wife and editor, and my daughter
Becca without whose advice and assistance this
would never have been published.

Chapter 1

"**D**ad says that the smoke on the horizon is where they live," said Cas, pointing to the faint trail of smoke on the distant horizon.

"I want to go there," said Pat. "After all, dad and mom used to live there in the tribe, which is really our tribe too."

"I know, but we can't just go there," said Cas. "Besides, dad has never told us anything about why they had to leave it in the first place, so it might be dangerous."

"Well, he did mention an attack by another tribe, so that must have had something to do with it," said Pat.

"He doesn't like to talk about it since mom is no longer with us," said Cas.

"I know, but I really want to go there," Pat repeated.

"But we can't just go there without asking," said Cas.

"Why not?" asked Pat. "We can do this. I'll take that six shooter that he gave me."

"Wait! What? He didn't give you any bullets, so I don't think he meant for you to actually use it," said Cas.

"I won't use it, I'll just take it," said Pat.

"Just for show?" asked Cas. "He said nobody but us even knows what a gun is for, so you're not likely to scare anyone just by carrying it since they have no idea what it's for."

"We don't know that for sure," said Pat.

"How could someone in a primitive tribe know what a gun looks like?" asked Cas.

"OK, but I'd feel safer with it," said Pat.

"Well, we shouldn't be going anyway since this could end up bad if we get into some kind of trouble there with the tribe," said Cas.

"We'll be on our horses, so we ride in, and if something goes wrong, we ride out," said Pat.

"Just ride out?....Oh my god, you're really serious about this aren't you," said Cas.

"Very much so," said Pat.

"Does this have anything to do with that noise and glow in the sky several days ago that came from where the smoke is?" asked Cas.

"Kind of, yes," said Pat. "OK, no, definitely yes."

"That could have been some kind of violence you know," said Cas.

"That's right, in fact that's exactly what I was thinking," said Pat.

"And that could be dangerous, so it's why you want to take the gun?" asked Cas.

"Look, I just want to know what's going on there," said Pat. "Maybe they need our help."

"Our help?" asked Cas wide eyed. "What can we do?"

"I don't know, but it's our tribe, so shouldn't we be able to do something?" asked Pat. Cas looked at him for awhile before speaking. She looked off in the distance at the smoke, then back at him.

"I suppose they really could need help if it had anything to do with that other tribe, like the one that attacked them and resulted in dad and mom moving here," she replied, finally.

"Look, Cas, after mom and dad discovered that time capsule and sealed vault, they learned how to read, and even speak," said Pat. "It awakened them, and then us, into a world that had nearly destroyed itself a long time ago. A world where humans had grown from just another animal to amazing greatness, only to become reduced to tribes like the one where mom and dad lived as primitives. Before they found the capsule, they were not aware of anything except survival in the wild. But the devices they found in the capsule taught them words and the talking box that you cranked taught them language and how to speak and pronounce words."

"Dad says that finding something like that was a very special gift from whoever left it," said Pat. "Because of what we now know, and what we are now capable of doing, is the reason I want to go to our tribe. What if they do need help and we're sitting here doing nothing?"

"OK, but what can a seventeen and eighteen year old do?" asked Cas.

"I don't know, but I think we at least have to go there and find out what's going on, and come home for help if we have to," said Pat. "Maybe we can even do something while we're there."

"And you want to go there carrying a gun without bullets?"

3

asked Cas.

"I'll ask him for the bullets," said Pat.

"Oh right, you'll ask him for bullets?" asked Cas. "And what do you think he'll say to that?"

"I don't know, but I actually think he might give them to me," said Pat.

"You know what he said about guns when he let you carry that one," said Cas.

"I know, but look, I've been thinking about doing this ever since that night we saw the glow in the sky," said Pat.

"So then why didn't you mention it to dad?" asked Cas.

"I don't know, maybe I should have," said Pat.

"So why not talk to him about that now?" asked Cas.

"He saw it too, and didn't say anything," said Pat.

"So you want to take matters into your own hands?" asked Cas.

"Well, yes, and we have those two horses we raised from young colts, so we can just ride out there and find out what happened," said Pat, pointing to a pair of orange and white paints in a makeshift corral down near the river that ran through the valley.

"So when did you want to do this?" she asked after a moment of thought.

"Tomorrow morning," said Pat.

"Wow, and you're sure we shouldn't ask dad first?" asked Cas.

"No," said Pat. "But when we come back we can tell him what we found."

"Right, tell him what we found," Cas repeated, looking first at the smoke on the horizon, and then at Pat without saying any more.

"So, are you in?" asked Pat.

4

"I don't know, I guess, unless we get caught trying," said Cas.

"Alright, then let's start quietly putting our plan into action," said Pat.

"Well, I really think we should talk with dad first, but I do agree with you that he would not let us go, and I am concerned about what might have happened to the tribe the other night." said Cas.

That evening, in the bunker where they were born and had lived ever since, they began planning their adventure. They would tell their dad it was just a horse ride around the valley which was something they often did in the mild climate where they lived. Occasionally, they would dress in some ancient clothing they found in the vault. For their adventure, they chose cowboy outfits, complete with cowboy hats and boots. The outfits were a bright cream color with sequins and leather frills. There was even a fancy holster for a six shooter which their father had found in the vault. Their father had also found some bullets, but they did not know where he kept them. They would tell him it was just a ride out in the valley, and Pat wanted to take the six shooter with him in that fancy holster. He also wanted to see how the bullets were placed in the gun, even though he would not go with bullets in the gun. It would be just another step in learning how to use the gun, which his father had said he would learn someday.

The next morning, clad in their cowboy outfits, Cas and Pat stood before their father.

"Wow, Roy Rogers and Dale Evans," said the father.

"Who were they?" asked Cas.

"Ancient folk heros," said the father. "I read about them in one of the books from the vault."

"We wanted to take the horses and go for a ride up the Valley," said Pat.

"You picked a nice day for it," said the father. "Oh, and since you're wearing that nice holster, you might want to put your Colt 45 in it." He reached behind him and held the pistol in his hand.

"Oh yeah, sure," said Pat, glancing quickly at Cas who just opened her eyes wide and shrugged.

"Does it have bullets?" asked Pat, as he looked it over.

"Of course, wait here," said the father who went back into the vault and returned with a handful of bullets. He then took the pistol from Pat, and one by one showed him how to place the bullets into the cylinder.

"Did you see how I did that?" asked the father.

"Yes, but It has six holes," said Pat.

"I know, but there were only five bullets," said the father who now handed Pat the gun. Pat carefully placed it in the holster.

"Can I keep them in the gun for the ride?" asked Pat.

"Sure, and when you get back I'll show you how to shoot," said the father. Pat said nothing but exchanged glances with Cas who was now smiling.

"I'll go down to the horses with you," said the father.

Outside, they went down to where the horse's were corralled and threw blankets from the vault over their backs. They then leaped on, much like the American Indians did many thousands of years ago. They waved to their father as they splashed across the river where it was shallow enough to cross. On the other side, they waved again to their father. As they rode, they occasionally looked back to make sure their father was going back into the bunker. When they saw that he had, they turned the horses South toward the forest and soon disappeared into the woods.

There were no trails on their way through the woods, but

6

eventually they came upon what might have been a road a thousand years or more ago. It was covered by a thick layer of soil, grass and brush. A few small trees were also present. But it was easier going for the horses compared to thrashing through the forest. After several hours they stopped. Pat looked at the little compass he had found in the vault to get his bearings. He pointed to their right and they left the road and after awhile climbed a gentle rise. As they came to the top, they could see movement ahead as well as the tops of crude structures. They stopped for a moment and waited to see if they had been noticed. All movement ahead had stopped. It was now eerily quiet. They waited. Pat had his hand on the handle of the pistol even though he had never fired it before and had no intention of using it.

"What do you think?" whispered Cas, finally.

"I don't know, should we just ride into the village?" he whispered.

"I don't know," she whispered back.

"Well, I'm not sure, but what else can we do since we're here?" he whispered back. "Besides, I think they know we're here because of the silence, and they haven't attacked us yet, so that's good."

"Haven't attacked us yet?" asked Cas now a little louder, looking at him with raised eyebrows.

"I have no idea what to expect," he whispered back.

"I know....but I'm sure we'll be quite a sight in these clothes and on horses," said Cas a bit louder.

"I know, but we're here," whispered Pat, holding his finger to his lips.

"Well, we can't turn around now without appearing to be running away, and if they are aggressive they might come after us," she whispered.

7

"Let's just go in," said Pat in a normal voice, taking the pistol out of his holster and giving his horse a little kick to go forward. She followed. They rode the remaining distance to the top of the rise and then started down the gentle slope through the trees toward a large open area surrounded by huts. There was a large rock fire pit in the middle with smoke rising into the blue morning sky. As they slowly rode into the open they could see dozens of animal-skin-clad people on their left near the huts, cowering back. Their faces were clearly in shock at what they were seeing. Ahead, at the far side of the clearing stood a large man, also in a skin, with a large hairy face. In one hand he carried a spear with a tip that looked like it was made of quartz. They continued slowly toward him and stopped a dozen or so feet away. He gritted his teeth and let out an angry shout while pounding the shank of the spear against the ground, but he did not move. Pat held the pistol at arm's length, aimed at the quartz tip, pulled back the hammer, and pulled the trigger. A loud bang and gush of blue smoke came from the gun. The recoil from the gun jolted Pat and he shut his eyes. Screams erupted from the crowd, and some tripped trying to retreat. When Pat opened his eyes, to his amazement, he had hit the tip, and it had shattered into a million pieces, showering the man with tiny quartz pellets that must have hurt since he shut his eyes and dropped the spear while covering his face with both hands. A loud groan came from the crowd, and those who were still on their feet, fell to their knees, others bowing to the two cowboys in the middle. The contrast between the nearly white-clad figures with white cowboy hats riding orange and white pinto horses, and the crowd of people clad in dark animal skins with dirty faces, could not have been more dramatic. As the smoke cleared, Cas and Pat sat motionless on their horses, waiting for some kind of response from the big man. There was none. He did not move. The crowd did not move. The big man just stood there with his hands at his side, holding his ground and glaring at them as if still on guard. They weren't sure if he would just continue to stand there or charge them, even though his spear was now just a long stick on the ground.

"I don't know, should we just leave?" asked Cas quietly. Hearing her voice, some in the crowd looked around as if to ask what she had said. They made sounds not resembling a language but it could have represented some form of communication.

"Well, first of all, we came here to see if we could help," said Pat.

"But then you shoot at the chief who seemed to be guarding the tribe," said Cas.

"I felt threatened," said Pat.

"I know, so did I, but I'm just recounting what we've done so far," said Cas.

"I expected a bigger tribe, and judging from the number of huts, there doesn't appear to be enough people," said Pat. "What do you think?"

"They all seem to be smaller than I was expecting, and from those whose bodies I can see inside the skins, they all seem to be women," said Cas.

"Yeah, I noticed that too," said Pat. "So something is clearly odd here, but I'm not sure what to do next."

"Here's what I think," said Cas. "If we just ride out of here after shooting at the chief and not making any attempt to make peace or show friendship, then how does that appear to be helping, which is why we came?" asked Cas.

"I know, but I think the damage is done regarding the chief," said Pat.

"I agree that the damage is done regarding him, but what about these women?" asked Cas.

"I'm not sure what to do, maybe we can ask them to follow us home?" asked Pat.

"Oh, right, I suppose…..uh….well, OK, maybe not, so for now, I guess, let's just calmly ride out the way we came and ask dad what to do next," said Cas."

"Alright, calmly, as in slow, as in we're not afraid," said Pat.

"I know, even though I am," said Cas, turning her horse and slowly riding back the way they came. Pat followed.

As they were beginning to leave the square, they could feel the movement of people behind them. They continued slowly riding out, not wanting to look back. But Pat finally glanced back and saw what had to be the entire tribe behind them.

"I think it's everyone, and they seem almost happy, so I wonder what that means?" asked Pat.

"Happy? Really?" asked Cas who now turned to see. She looked over at Pat and shut her eyes tightly in a gesture that seemed to say 'what in the hell is going on?'

"I shouldn't have shot the chief's spear tip," said Pat. "But, I must say, it was a good shot considering it was my first."

"Well, you're right, it was a good shot, and nobody actually got hurt too badly," said Cas as they reached the top of the rise where they stopped for a moment. Behind them, the tribe came to a stop in a non-threatening group well clear of them. All eyes were upon them.

"I think they like us, so maybe we should at least wave to them," said Pat. Cas nodded. They both turned their horses sideways and waved to them, with smiles on their faces. The crowd responded with many strange noises, corresponding smiles, and some laughter, while waving with their arms in the air.

"Primitives smile, laugh and grunt their speech, but we know what they mean," said Cas.

"That's because they're just like you and me but without an education," said Pat. "I just wonder if I did them a favor by knocking their chief down a notch or two."

"Maybe, but more importantly, I'm wondering why the entire tribe is only made up of women?" asked Cas.

"The men might be out hunting," said Pat.

"Not all of the men, and also where are the children?" asked Cas. "No men, no children.....Something is definitely wrong here."

"And it really doesn't look like the chief is even related to either us or the women," said Pat.

"I agree, so that's another odd thing here," said Cas.

"But we can't do anything about all of the oddness now, even though we know it's definitely not right. So let's go back home and tell dad what's going on here, because I think he will want to know what we found and may very well want to follow up on the situation," said Pat.

"Yes, I think dad will definitely want to know about this, and, yes again, I know he'll want to do something," said Cas.

"But what can we do?" asked Pat.

"Let's talk to him and we'll figure something out," said Cas.

"Alright, let's get going," said Pat.

With that they turned and started back home. It was nearly dark when they entered the valley. In the distance, standing near the entrance to the bunker, was their father. He stood with his hands on his hips until they were beginning to dismount near the wooden gate that they had fashioned for the crude corral where the horses lived. By now he had started down toward them. As he approached they could tell he was not happy. They had rehearsed the story they would tell him on their way back, but once he was standing in front of them Cas found that she could not lie to him, and looked at Pat for help. Pat just shook his head. Their father saw him do that and turned to Cas.

"Well, what did you do?" he asked accusingly without a trace of anger.

"We rode to your old tribal village," said Cas.

"And what happened there?" he asked, still in a calm voice.

"Well, we came face to face with what we assume was their chief, but he really didn't look like any of the tribe," said Pat.

"How so?" asked the father.

"He was bigger, hairier, and with a different face," said Cas.

"So what did you do?" asked the father.

"Well, the chief had a spear with this shiny, sharp tip," said Pat.

"And what did you do?" asked the father.

"I shot the tip off of his spear," said Pat.

"You shot at him?" asked the father, now showing a little anger.

"I felt threatened and just reacted," said Pat.

"But at least you aimed at his spear, not at him," said the father.

"That's right, and nobody was really hurt," said Pat.

"So what did this chief do after that?" asked the father.

"Nothing, he just stood his ground and looked at us," said Cas.

"I know it was wrong, and I shouldn't have fired the gun," said Pat.

"What did the tribe do after that?" asked the father.

"They seemed happy and followed us out," said Cas. "But there's something very wrong there."

12

"Oh, and what's that?" asked the father.

"From what we can tell, they were all women, and there were no men or children," said Cas. "I didn't even see older women."

"Many of the men could have been out hunting, but not all of the men, and there were no children which makes no sense at all," said the father. "You're right, something is very wrong, and likely bad."

"One of the things we wanted to find out was whether that glow in the sky we saw the other evening would have had anything to do with this," said Pat.

"And we think what we found says it most likely did," said Cas.

"Obviously it must have," said the father. "I should have been as curious about that as you two were."

"We felt we had to find out," said Pat.

"I should have been the one who raised the question," said the father.

"Well, it is what it is, and we did what we did," said Pat.

"I'm also curious about the so called chief you saw, since my tribe really didn't have anything like that when I lived there," said the father. "However, I do recall another tribe that I had seen while out with our hunting party. The men in that party seem to fit your description. I believe we called them Gorfs."

"Gorfs?" asked Pat. "Like I said, he was bigger uglier and hairier."

"Yes, I think that's a Gorf," said the father.

"My opinion is that he was guarding the tribe, even if he wasn't their chief," said Cas.

"I agree with Cas, because he yelled and slammed his spear on the ground to challenge us and try to scare us away," said Pat.

"Interesting, and you said the women were smiling and laughing after you shot at him and then were leaving?" he asked.

"Yes, I thought they wanted to follow us home," said Pat.

"Yes, right then and there," said Cas.

"Well, something is definitely not right if there were only women and there was a Gorf standing guard over the women," said the father.

"You know what, those women were so nice, and I want to see them again," said Cas.

"I think that's a very good idea, and we should do that right away," said the father.

"You mean for them to come here to live?" asked Cas.

"Yes, to live," he replied. "They're our tribe after all, and they're not really savages, they're just us without access to the knowledge that we have had the opportunity to learn. They're merely uneducated humans."

"I know that, but when you see them, they don't look or act like us until you see them smile and laugh. Then it's like you just want to hug them," said Cas.

"Alright, so let's recap what you did," said the father. "You ride into a village of people who have never seen anything like you before, and you're dressed like Roy Rogers and Dale Evans in your white outfits. Then you shoot their guard's spear. Immediately after that, you ride out and they follow you like they want to come with you. Is that pretty much what happened?"

"That's exactly what happened," said Pat.

"I think what you did was something very good, and something we needed to do, despite my lack of attention to it," said the father. "And it was very timely since that glow in the sky the other evening had to be an attack on the village. So now, knowing what we know,

14

I think we have to act, and act quickly."

"I know, I felt guilty just leaving them there," said Pat. "They need us."

"That's right, they do need us, because they're still in danger," said the father. "Also, I think you just made friends with them, which is a very good thing,"

"Yes, I agree, they do see us as friends," said Cas. "I could see it in their eyes."

"It turns out that your little visit was not only timely, but necessary, despite the fact that I would never have approved it," said the father. "The fact that the tribe had only women is very bad, so we need to find out what happened, and right away. Then we have to do something about it, also right away. It seems probable that the Gorf was in fact guarding the women against another tribe that was responsible for the missing men and children."

"So then the Gorf chief is on our side?" asked Pat.

"I'm pretty sure, yes," said the father.

"So how do we get the women to come here?" asked Cas.

"Well, in my opinion, they'll come here on their own, and I think they'll come right away based on what you saw as you left."

"Oh, I hope so," said Cas. "I want to hug every one of them."

"Why do you think they'll come right away?" asked Pat.

"For one thing they might see Roy Rogers and Dale Evans as the tribe's new protectors," said the father. "And for another, I think they might just want to get away from that place because of what's happened there."

"I can totally understand wanting to get away from there, because it's what I would want to do," said Cas.

"But what about the Gorf who was in fact guarding them?" asked Pat.

15

"I want him to come here with them to live with us," said the father.

"Do you think he'll come?" asked Pat.

"From your description, he seemed to be a very dedicated guard, and as such he will likely accompany the women here when they come," said the father.

"I hope so, because I feel so guilty for what I did," said Pat.

"You did what you felt was right at the time, so let's just see what happens," said the father.

"I just want the women to be here now," said Cas.

"I know, but I think they'll be here soon," said the father. "Listen, surviving in the wild is not easy, and having an enemy to worry about while you are trying to survive might drive them to do something they might not otherwise do on the spur of the moment, like pulling up stakes and moving to a safer place with what they might assume are their new friends and protectors," said the father.

"So then let's figure out where they will stay when they get here," said Cas.

"I agree, but it's late, so we'll do that first thing in the morning," said the father as he turned to go into the bunker.

"I'm curious about what that other tribe would do with our tribe's men and children," said Cas as they sat around the table and chairs the father had found in the vault years ago.

"So am I," said the father. "And I'm sure we just put ourselves into the middle of something very big. I'm also sure we'll be in it to the end, whatever that may turn out to be."

"I hope it's something good," said Cas.

"We'll make it something good," said the father.

"Dad, I know I did wrong by not discussing this with you

16

first," said Pat. "But you wouldn't have let us go."

"You're right, I wouldn't have," said the father, as he leaned against a post and closed his eyes for a moment. "And by not talking to me first you two probably saved our tribe from who knows what terrible fate."

"I just hope it will turn out to be something positive," said Pat.

"I think it will, but we have to do something, and do it quickly," said the father. "Our tribe is in crisis, and we must step up to help them."

"First is get the women here," said Cas.

"And then protect them from this other tribe with our guns," said the father.

"Then what?" asked Pat. "Do we go after that other tribe?"

"Getting the women here and protecting them, yes," said the father. "Going after the other tribe, no."

"Are you sure the women will know the way here, or do we need to go there and get them?" asked Cas

"All tribal members know the way to just about everything within many miles of the tribe. It's their hunting ground, and they know how to track prey, so they can easily track two horses," said the father.

"But the women don't hunt, so they may not know all of that, do they?" asked Cas.

"The women forage for food, pick berries and other edibles, and get firewood," said the father. "So they wander far and wide to do that."

"But we've never seen them here before," said Cas.

"That's because our Valley has likely been considered a place to avoid from something I did long ago," said the father.

"What did you do?" asked Pat.

"I had to shoot and kill one of them," said the father.

"You shot someone?" asked Cas.

"He was trying to take your mother and I wasn't able to stop him any other way," said the father. "The other men who were with him ran, and we've never seen anyone from the tribe come here since."

"So then maybe the women won't come either," said Cas.

"I think fear of this other tribe will overcome any fear of coming, particularly after they saw you shoot the tip off their guard's spear," said the father. "But I suspect they will hesitate before they actually enter the Valley, so we need to be on the lookout, so we can invite them in if we see them."

"I'll be watching closely," said Cas.

"The men of your tribe hunted deer like you?" asked Pat.

"Yes, and antelope, and pigs," said the father.

"How can they hunt without a rifle like yours?" asked Pat.

"They hunt on foot with spears," said the father.

"But the deer and antelope are very fast," said Pat.

"Well, if they can wound one, they just run them down until they drop," said the father.

"Wait, run down an antelope?," said Pat.

"Oh yes, humans are two-legged animals, and two-legged animals are more efficient at running than four-legged animals despite the fact that most four-legged animals are much faster over shorter distances. I just read that in a book, and it's something I absolutely did not know. Apparently, over long distances, a two-legged animal can chase down a four-legged animal until they drop, especially if they've been able to wound it."

"That is amazing, I never would have imagined that," said Pat.

"So how long do we wait if the women don't show up right

18

away?" asked Cas.

"Don't worry, I think they'll be here in the morning," said the father.

"So, if they're not here by then, do we go get them?" asked Cas.

"That's right, what if they're afraid to come on their own?" asked Pat.

"Look, I think you two have inadvertently made it a lot easier for them to want to come here because you gave them a destination, which was something they did not have before," said the father.

"If that other tribe comes instead, or is coming after them, we have guns," said Pat, patting his pistol.

"Yes, but with very limited ammo," said the father. "So it's just temporary, because when we run out of ammo, we're back to primitive defense, and right now we have very little of that since I've relied on guns up to now."

"I know, so we'll have to use them sparingly," said Pat. "I only have four bullets left."

"Look, I've read most of the books in our library," said the father. "Guns are just one weapon in an evolution of weapons from spears to thermonuclear bombs and other weapons of mass destruction. So, if you read about the evolution of mankind, you see conflict among tribes over hunting territory and then progressively over a whole host of other things. In those conflicts, each new generation of humans has produced increasingly more powerful weapons, not to hunt for food, but to kill one another. So why is this particular period we live in any different? It isn't. We're all humans and we seem to have a penchant to fight like animals, but in our case we are smarter than animals. So we can do things that animals cannot do, and that's build increasingly more deadly weapons for killing

19

our human enemies. And eventually, the concept of victory begins to exceed merely the defeat of our enemies, but the necessity to eradicate them entirely. And once the nuclear age reached a critical mass of fully armed enemies, it created the potential for the mass annihilation of all fellow humans. It raised the possibility of ending human life on the planet entirely. The war that erupted became what some called a scorched earth, in which no one wins and everyone loses, including the ecosystem needed to support life."

"But we only have a few guns and very few bullets, so it's not as if we're starting that whole thing over again," said Cas.

"I know, but I just want you to understand what happened in the past with weapons like the guns we have," said the father.

"I understand, but we have them, and right now we need them to protect ourselves," said Pat.

"OK, but I just wanted you to know about our past history with weapons and how things can escalate once we start using them again," said the father.

"I realize that humans have this penchant, as you say, but in our situation now with these women, I'm not sure I'm that concerned about what happened in the past," said Cas.

"Well, women are also human and capable of acting in the same way as men," said the father. "However in this case, I think I agree with you, and I'm not really concerned about them seeking to acquire our guns. And even though I have wanted to keep our guns a secret, I'm afraid now, faced with protecting the safety of our tribe, and ourselves, we will have to use them."

"Actually, dad, since you shot someone in the process of making this valley forbidden, you've already broken your rule of secrecy," said Pat.

"You're right, I did," said the father.

20

"So let's say that what I did can be just one event and not an arms race," said Pat.

"Well, there is a symbolic event I've read about called Pandora's Box," said the father. "It suggests that once you have let some secret out of the box, it is forever out of the box and the situation cannot be reversed."

"Meaning there's nothing we can do about what's happened, including your shooting a man?" asked Pat.

"That's true," said the father. "Humans are very intelligent, even ones you may have considered to be just mindless savages like those you saw in the village. But don't underestimate humans regardless of what you may think of them in their present state. In the distant past we were often naive enough, once we had achieved enormous wealth, power and achievements, to believe that the ignorant masses were inferior to us. Only to find out they too are humans just like everyone else, and just as smart as those at the top of the heap."

"But those women we saw in the village haven't acquired the knowledge that we have, they're at the very beginning," said Pat.

"That's true, but do not underestimate fellow humans," said the father. "Look, we are all Homo Sapiens and capable of amazingly intelligent things. We are also very clever and cunning if the situation calls for it. Your mother and I were no different than those you saw in the village today, and with the devices we were given we were able to gradually unlock the secrets contained in the time capsule and vault."

"I think you called it a miracle," said Pat.

"In my mind, it was, but we were humans, and smart enough to figure it out," said the father.

"OK, so with all of that background in mind, we have a

challenge before us, and that's preparing for the women to come here," said Cas."

"And after that, an even greater challenge: to find those who did this to our tribe and then try to get our men and children back," said Pat.

"Yes, we do have to take that one on, even though right now I have no idea how we'll be able to do it," said the father.

"But it's still one we must take on," said Cas.

"I know," said the father.

"So, the women come here and we become a tribe again," said Cas. "I'm sure this other tribe is not through with us, so let's say they come here. We shoot them with our guns. Then what? How do we get our men and children back?"

"We organize a posse of mostly women and attack the other tribe with our guns," said Pat.

"Uh, right, and when we run out of bullets in the middle of that very interesting battle?" asked the father.

"OK, so that may not be the best plan," said Pat.

"Maybe we can move away from here," said Cas.

"To where?" asked the father. "And if we do move, what happens to our men and children? Whatever we do in the short term, we have to be able to defend, as well as feed and care for these women. Keep in mind that feeding a tribe is much more difficult than you think, especially considering that we're just able to feed ourselves. Remember, we will, in many ways, be just another village trying to survive in a very demanding natural environment. We could be eaten by a mountain lion just like any other animal, because we're just food to them."

"I never thought of it that way because we have guns to shoot them with," said Pat.

"And when the bullets run out, we're just like any primitive human," said the father.

"I know," said Pat.

"Well, I think right now we have to just focus on the challenge that's before us," said Cas. "And that's accommodating the women."

"That's right, and for me what matters is how these women view us," said the father. "Will they see us as family, or just strangers trying to help. It's been a long time since I lived in the tribe, and I have no idea if there is any resentment toward me personally for running away."

"Dad, that was a long time ago, and none of these women will even know anything about it, so don't worry about that," said Cas.

"You're probably right, so I guess we really can't worry about that or anything else. We have to just welcome them as if they are our own, and then deal with this other tribe when we have to."

"Yes, and I can't wait for them to be here," said Cas.

"I can't either," said the father. "But now, we need to get some sleep so we can be fresh in the morning."

Chapter 2

The next morning they sat around the table in the bunker discussing their plan for the day which would be focused on accommodating the women from their tribe.

"So, do we each arm ourselves with a gun just in case we encounter this other tribe?" asked Cas.

"Yes, I think it would be a good idea," said the father. "This other tribe might be keeping close tabs on our tribe, and what you did yesterday might get them to take some kind of action. So we need to be prepared for that.

"Dad, you say that all the guns have some bullets?" asked Pat.

"Four of them do, and the rifle with silencer and scope that I use for hunting has the most," he replied.

"I forgot, why do you need a silencer for hunting?" asked Cas.

"Because firing a shot without a silencer would be heard for miles and would scare away what is our food supply," he replied.

"Oh right," she responded, slapping the side of her head.

"If the women don't come and we have to go to the tribe to escort them back here, we have only two horses, so who would go?" asked Cas.

"Let's not get into that until we know they're not coming," said the father. "Look, I think they'll come right away, so just be patient."

"That's the hard part," said Cas.

"You just left there yesterday mid-day, so it hasn't been that long," said the father. "Let's talk about who gets which gun."

"I already have the 45," said Pat.

"You keep that, and there's one other pistol," said the father. "Cas will have that one. It's smaller and can even fit in a pocket."

"I don't have a pocket," said Cas.

"It's in a pouch so you can carry it in that," said the father.

"So, you'll have your rifle?" asked Pat.

"No, I'll take the shotgun, because I don't want to waste my hunting ammo because I'm starting to run low on it," said the father.

"Which one is the shotgun?" asked Pat.

"This one," said the father, holding it up.

"Wow, two big barrels," said Pat.

"It looks more like a cannon than a gun," said Cas.

"Instead of a bullet, the shells are filled with a lot of beebees, and the farther you are from the target the wider the spray of beebees," said the father holding up one of the shells.

"So then it can't kill a person, does it just spray them with beebees?" asked Pat.

25

"Oh no, it can definitely kill someone at close range with just about any size beebee, but the shells we have are loaded with buckshot, so the beebees are fairly big," said the father. "So it can do a lot of damage even a ways away, but it's definitely not for long range like the rifle."

"So it has a limited range," said Pat.

"Yes, but so do your pistols, especially the one Cas has," said the father.

"But we still have the rifle for long range if we need it," said Pat.

"Of course," said the father. "So let's go outside in case the women show up."

The three of them went outside and sat on the grass.

"I'm just glad we have the guns," said Cas.

"Yeah, me too," said Pat. "I just wonder if other parts of the world have been able to find guns like we did."

"Unfortunately, we have no idea what's going on in other parts of the world," said the father. "It could actually be ultra modern in some areas if they were able to avoid the nuclear conflagration."

"Or perhaps the entire world is a vast wasteland and not more advanced than here," said Cas.

"That's right, we could even be the last people surviving on the planet," said Pat.

"Well, I doubt that," said the father. "We don't even know how long ago it happened. It could have been thousands of years. We have no reference date, and the books in the vault are from a specific era, but we have no idea how long ago that was. So if it's thousands of years, some areas that were destroyed may well have been able to recover by now. Other parts may have completely survived the devastation and be ultra modern. We just don't know. It's a very big world."

"What about those who left the time capsule?" asked Cas.

"Something else we don't know," said the father. "Assuming they survived the war and saw the result in person, it may have been a lifelong ambition to leave a legacy for someone in the distant future to find. "They would have known that many people retreated into the wilderness to survive off the land with little or no resources, and that they might eventually end up like our tribe as primitives, needing a hand up to be able to carry on the human presence. The other thing I suspect is that while those who left our capsule may have survived, their future might have been limited, so they believed the end for them was near. These people were very far thinking and noble. Because the very idea of saving the great accomplishments of mankind for future generations so that it will not have been lost forever is a priceless gift to those who would eventually find it."

"It was a priceless gift to us, and we can pass this knowledge on to others," said Cas. "In fact, I will take each of these women as students and fill their minds with the wealth of knowledge that we were given."

"Very good Cas, because I know that's what the people who left the vault and capsule would want," said the father.

"I can't wait for them to be able to tell us their story," said Cas.

"We clearly have a lot to do after they get here," said the father.

"Including moving from here?" asked Cas.

"I know, I've thought a lot about that," said the father. "I've studied maps, and the Pacific Ocean is no more than a days

27

journey from here. We could move there if we came under siege from this other tribe. Or we could just move there in anticipation of hostilities. I'm sure it would be a more abundant hunting ground for us."

"The ocean does seem like a good place to search for food, as well as perhaps meet other tribes that are not hostile," said Pat.

"Of course we'd have to take as much of what we can from the vault," said the father.

"We have two horses to help carry things," said Cas.

"Maybe I could go there by myself to scout it out," said Pat.

"Don't get any ideas son," said the father. "This is far more complicated than just a horse ride adventure."

"Right, I guess we need to stick together now that we have the women to think about," said Pat.

Cas suddenly stood up and pointed. Across the river emerging cautiously from the trees were two women. When Cas saw them, she waved to them with both hands. The two quickly waved back and let out cries that could be heard all the way to where they were. Then, from the woods came a flood of women and soon the entire tribe was running toward the river, carrying armloads of things. The minute Cas saw them start for the river, she did the same, followed by Pat and the father. The women stopped on the opposite bank just as Cas and Pat reached their side. The father was last to arrive. The women were literally jumping up and down waving as shreeks of joy filled the air.

"They did come like you said," said Cas, as she now pointed to the shallows in the river and began walking toward it, waving for the women to follow. They saw what she was pointing at and the entire tribe began rushing toward it.

"They're so excited to see us," said the father in amazement as he hustled to follow Cas and Pat toward the shallows.

"I'll meet them halfway across," said Cas, who was running as fast as she could while continuing to wave toward the shallows.

"They must have camped in the woods last night!" shouted the father as he tried to keep pace with Cas and Pat.

"I know," Pat shouted back. "It must have taken them all yesterday afternoon and part of the night to walk here from their village carrying those bundles. Yes, they literally followed you two after you left yesterday."

"They seem to be carrying some of what they'll need to live here," said Pat as he arrived at the shallows. Cas was already halfway across when Pat and the father got there.

The first few women to arrive at the shallows knew exactly what to do. Before long, the river was filled with the women carrying their armloads of things. Cas met the first woman and took her arm to help her to the other side where she threw her things to the ground. Cas then hugged her tightly, then turned to greet the rest as they trudged as fast as they could to get across. Soon, they were all on the other side where they dropped their things on the ground. The day before, Cas had found a place for their new camp. She now motioned for them to follow as she led them to a stand of trees not far up the valley. In the middle of the stand was a large clearing that was now lit by the morning sun. It did not take long before all of them were inside the space where their noisy chatter continued unabated. Cas then went to the center where she and Pat had already built a small fire pit. She pointed to it, then looked around for another rock and picked it up to place on the side, then pointed to the pit. Immediately others were looking for rocks and before long a very large fire pit had been built while others were gathering up wood. Their father

29

was now at one side of the clearing watching with a smile that was ear to ear.

"Cas?" he shouted over the chatter. "Let's get them settled here and I'll head out to bag a deer or antelope, and we'll serve a midday meal for our guests!" He then turned to head back into the bunker to retrieve his rifle.

"They weren't able to bring a lot, but of course they just picked up what they could carry and came," said Pat. "I'll help them carry their things up here."

"Let's both start to do that and watch them follow us," said Cas. She pointed down to the river and started following Pat. The hint was enough because the entire tribe was on their heels by the time they reached the field of packs. Everyone had an armload as they carried them back to the new camp where each woman found a place in the grass to settle down. It was not long before the clearing began to look like a real camp.

The happiness among the women was obvious, and the unintelligible chatter and laughter continued to fill the air. Across the river, at the edge of the forest where the women had emerged, stood the chief, hesitant to come forward. Cas finally spotted him and ran back to the shallows where she waded across. She quickly made her way to where the chief was standing. As she drew near, she smiled at him and pointed to where the women were setting up camp. A number of the women were now waving to them, and she waved back. She then turned to the chief and motioned for him to follow. At first he hesitated, but finally he followed, and by the time Cas reached the river to cross, the chief was right there beside her. As they approached the stand of trees where the women were getting settled, several had come out to welcome him. By now the fire pit was ablaze. The chief was clearly happy to be with them and it wasn't long before he took up a position at the edge where he stood as if on guard.

Over the next hour or so, Cas took some of them to show them how to use what was referred to as their 'outhouse' which was a big hole in the ground inside a cluster of bushes not far away. Over the hole was an elevated platform of logs with a footrest where they could go to the bathroom. From the odor that now permeated the campsite, she assumed correctly that none of them had ever really bathed. So she retrieved several soap bars from the vault and summoned a half dozen of them to follow her to the river. She and Pat bathed almost daily in the river and she was going to make sure the women did the same. The little group assembled near the shallows and Cas stripped off, took a bar of soap and stepped into the shallows, then went out where it was deep enough to begin washing herself. She then rinsed off and came ashore. She motioned for them to take off their skins, which they did immediately and went into the river like she did. They were soon trading the soap and laughing. It was not long before all the women came down and were there in the river which was soon filled with women splashing one another as they sudsed themselves. After awhile, Cas waved them ashore where they stood around in the nude waiting to dry off. It was not long before they were all back in their skins.

The climate was mild and mostly sunny year round in the valley, so bathing in the river provided the perfect opportunity to deal with the problem of body odor. Hygiene would continue to be high on Cas's priority list as she began to introduce them into what would be an entirely new life. One where they would eventually meet with others she considered civilized, to match pictures she had seen in books she had read.

"We have a ways to go to educate these women on a whole host of subjects, including other aspects of hygiene," said Pat when Cas finally jointed him at the edge of the camp.

"The women had never done very much about any of this throughout their lives, so this is totally new, but I think they love it," said Cas. "In their village, they simply were used to the smells, which for them was just part of daily life. Of course they must have had holes where they peed and pooped, but as far as anything else, probably not much. From now on, however, we will try to run a clean and odor free camp."

"We also need to set up a school somewhere to teach them as much as we know about everything, especially reading and language," said Pat. "We'll use the talking device and all the other props from the capsule and teach them in groups, like a school. "We need to be able to communicate with one another as soon as possible."

"We might also have to figure out how to build some kind of housing for them since they only brought a few things with them," said Cas. "It does rain here and gets cool, even cold some nights of the year."

"I know, but building housing could be a tall order," said Pat. "I guess we have nothing but time, but we'll need time since we have a million other things to do now that we have a village to care for."

"Well, if we were bored before, this should keep us busy for a long time," she replied.

"I know, we don't need to find who else is out there in the world when we have our own population right here," said Pat. "And, oh, did you notice what the chief actually looks like?"

"What do you mean?" she replied. "He has that animal skin

cape over him so I can't really see his body."

"He had it off for awhile and he looks a little bit like one of those pictures we saw of a Neanderthal of forty thousand years ago," said Pat. "But taller and without the hunched back. It seems to me he's just another one of us with Neanderthal-like features, nothing more."

"I know, he's just a larger, hairier human," said Cas. "And he seems like a very nice man, and the women like him a lot."

"I know, but I think I need to talk to dad about him," said Pat.

"That's right, we need to find out what he knows about the men and children that are missing," said Cas.

"Exactly, now let's get back to the question of housing for the women," said Pat. "I think that's at the top of our priority list."

"Right, I guess that has to be near the top of our list, next to how to feed everyone, considering the fact that we struggle to feed ourselves," said Cas. "Dad is out bagging a deer for now, but we have a lot of mouths to feed on a daily basis, and that won't be easy."

"OK, so here's what I'm thinking about housing," said Pat. "Dad believes that where we live now in that bunker is just a small part of a very large building that once existed prior to the war and is now buried under decades of dirt."

"So then it has rooms to live in?" asked Cas.

"That's what I'm thinking," said Pat. "He said we need to explore the interior and see if we can find other entrances. Then we might be able to convert parts of it into a shelter for the women," said Pat.

"I like that idea, but I'm still concerned that this is not the entire tribe, so what are we going to do when it expands once we get the men and children back?" asked Cas.

"I know, to say nothing about defending ourselves against attacks by that other tribe," said Pat. "But our immediate priority today is getting these women settled and fed."

"Yes," said Cas.

"However, in our spare time we can at least check out the possibility of finding rooms in that building," said Pat. "We can even do that at night. Dad has up to now limited how far we can go into the bunker, but now we have a reason to go farther. So we're going to have to take that oil lantern and go in a lot deeper, and I'm sure dad will agree to that."

"I know he will, and there are a few areas on the hill where the ground has caved in and those might be windows or doors, so they'll be good places to start," she replied.

"We have a load of other things to do now with these women, but we can at least spend a little time checking this out," said Cas.

"We'll discuss it with dad this evening after we eat," said Pat.

Their father returned with a deer that he had shot. It was draped over the back of a horse. The women knew exactly what to do with it, and that afternoon, they roasted it over the fire and everyone ate. Day one with the women and the chief ended with everyone going to sleep with a full stomach. But the next few weeks would be very busy for everyone. The women knew how to forage for food and much of each day was spent doing that. This was a supplement to the meat the father was still able to bring home from farther and farther away. At camp, Cas began teaching the women how to read and speak, as well as reminding them daily about the basics of hygiene. Pat and their father began to excavate an area that appeared to be the corner of the building. With the help of the chief who was as strong as two men, they were able to remove enough soil and debris to expose the side of a concrete structure that included a door and a large window whose glass was a little distorted but still intact. After managing to get the door open, they explored inside. The large room was empty, the floor littered with dust and debris. Through two adjoining doors, using the oil lantern, they found hallways and more rooms, but as they went deeper the need for more natural light became clearer. Their father suggested that they excavate around other windows to let in more light. The windows, once opened from the inside, could be located outside, making it easier to clear away the dirt to let the sun shine in. Cas decided that the building would be an apartment complex for the women but they would not be able to move in until she was sure they could live inside safely and cleanly. Their hygiene would have to be such that they could live together, odor free. Otherwise, the rooms could become a smelly pigpens.

It would take several months before Cas and Pat were able to teach the women how to pronounce a few words that describe things. Bathing, and brushing their teeth using the supply of dental supplies from the vault, was now becoming routine. It was not long before they began to understand why. Modern hygiene was not natural for them, but the elimination of odors, as well as cleanliness, made it worthwhile for everyone. Odor was something they had become accustomed to in the wild, but eliminating it was becoming something they found both necessary and comfortable to live with. And there was nothing like warm weather to make it easier and more fun to bathe.

The move into the apartments was progressing well and Cas was able to move some of them in. There were eleven rooms once several extra windows were uncovered, so it would be at least three to a room. The women were able to choose their roommates so that made it easier for them to adjust to living together.

Now, with many more mouths to feed, the father was beginning to reach a limit to what he was able to hunt for. The number of animals were becoming scarce, and he had to travel farther and farther away to find his prey. So thoughts of moving to the coast returned to their conversation. Aside from the meat he was able to bring home, the chief and the women were skilled at gardening, and some had brought seeds that they had used back at their old village to grow a few varieties of vegetables. They had gardens at their old village, so this was not new to them, and they were able to start and maintain a garden that the women watered from the river in buckets found in the vault. Within a month or so, the gardens were beginning to be productive, but they still needed the meat for protein. Despite all of their efforts, getting enough food was now becoming a central issue for them.

The chief had been Cas's student, and one day the father decided to try to question him about what he knew regarding the missing men, children and elderly which they desperately wanted to find and get back.

"Where are the others like you?" he first asked, pointing to chief's face and large muscular arms. The chief seemed a bit confused at first, but eventually grasped what the question was about.

"Eesst," he replied, pointing East up the valley where the river disappeared around a bend. It was where the father hunted, but he had never seen any sign of a village.

"How far?" asked the father.

"No far," he replied. East, the father thought, and not far? But where? He had often traveled several miles in that direction

36

and there was no sign of a village.

"Where did the other tribe take the men and children?" asked the father.

"They no keep, we take," said the chief, pointing East.

"Wait, your tribe has our men and children?" asked the father.

"Da!" said the chief emphatically.

"In your village?" asked the father.

"Da," said the chief, pointing and nodding. His tribe has our men and children! So apparently his tribe stopped this other tribe from completing whatever they were trying to do.

"Where is this other tribe that took our men and children?" asked the father.

"Der," said the chief, pointing South toward the father's old village. Right, the other tribe is South, obviously beyond his tribe. That makes sense, thought the father.

"The children and men are safe?" asked the father.

"Da, safe," said the chief. So the Gorfs now have the kidnapped members of his tribe and they are safe. The other tribe kidnapped them, and the Gorfs interceded and took them away from that tribe, and they're now keeping them. So why haven't they tried to return them? And do they know that the chief is guarding the women of his tribe?

"Does your tribe know where we are?" asked the father using gestures.

"Da," said the chief.

"Can they return the men and children to us?" asked the father.

"Other tribe attack," said the chief.

"So they can't leave without being attacked?" asked the father.

37

"Da," said the chief. OK, they're pinned down, thought the father.

"Why did the other tribe take the children?" asked the father.

"To teach diff..rent," said the chief. So, to make sure they were taught their way? Interesting, thought the father. His tribe was not being taught any beliefs, just survival skills, so what this other tribe is teaching is some kind of belief. If that's the case, this other tribe must be able to speak and read, thought the father. But is it a different language?

"Does other tribe speak like me?" asked the father.

"Da, speak, but not like you," said the chief. That's it then, thought the father, they're teaching them whatever they believe, whatever that is, in their language. Then this other tribe is apparently out recruiting people to teach whatever they believe.

"Why were the men taken?" asked the father.

"They defend women and children, so must be taken," said the chief. "They can be taught too, then become their warriors."

"Oh, wow," said the father. Right, just indoctrinate the men to become part of their tribe.

"What about the women, what did they want to do with them?" asked the father.

"Take for own, raise more children to teach their way," said the chief.

"And you stopped them?" asked the father.

"Da!" said the chief emphatically.

"What about the old people?" asked the father.

"Kill," said the chief.

"Kill? Why?" asked the father.

"No can teach, no use anymore," said the chief.

"Wow, this tribe is nothing short of evil," said the father.

"Da," said the chief.

The father could now see why the chief was the protector of the women. It was his job to keep this other tribe from taking the women for their own. And his tribe took the men and children to their village for safe keeping. They are now essentially trapped there by this other tribe. So the Gorfs are a friendly tribe. They are more than that. They are almost like his own tribe, thought the father. He could now see what was going on. This other tribe was that tribe referenced in the time capsule. A tribe intent on wanting to convert others to their belief. But they were not able to convert the Gorfs. And not only that, the Gorf's had come to the assistance of his tribe by intercepting the kidnapped tribal members, and are now holding them for safe keeping. But they feel they would be under siege if they tried to move the kidnapped people.

"Is your tribe safe from this other tribe?" he asked.

"Da, but must guard all the time," he replied with a nod.

"Good man," said the father, smiling broadly and patting the chief on the shoulder. The chief smiled and nodded.

So maybe when some of the women are able to converse with me I might find out more, thought the father. He desperately wanted to interview one or more of the women of his tribe. Cas has said that a few of them are beginning to learn words and she can carry on a conversation with at least one of them. Any new details could be important, so he needed to talk with one of them.

"I'd like to interview the woman you said you were able to talk with," said the father after he found Cas in the apartment complex getting four women settled in their new apartment.

"Sure, this evening I'll go down to the camp where the rest of the women are and I'll meet you there," she replied. He nodded

39

and that evening he went down to the camp. After awhile, Cas came in with one of the women.

"This is Sue," said Cas, turning to gesture to the woman who was with her. She was dressed in an orange jumper that Cas had made for her, and her hair was cut short like many of the women.

"Hi Sue," said the father, bowing slightly as he took her hand.

"You are father," said Sue. He sat back in surprise and looked at Cas with his eyes open wide.

"Um, yes," he replied with a smile at how well she pronounced the words.

"Sue can try to answer your questions," said Cas, pointing to a bench fashioned out of some logs and rocks. They sat down and the father turned to face Sue.

"I want to ask you a few questions about life in your village," he said.

"Yes," she nodded.

"It's about the other tribe who came to take your children away," he began.

"Sue said it happened at night," said Cas.

"So you've already discussed this with the women?" asked the father.

"I did, and none of them ever really saw the men very clearly," said Cas.

"So the men came at night and just took the children?" he asked, looking at Sue.

"Yes," said Sue.

"What about your men, where were they when this was taking place?" asked the father.

"There was a big fight outside and when it was over, I think the men were gone, at least I didn't hear them after that," said Sue.

The father's mouth was agape as he looked at Cas after listening to how well Sue spoke.

"She's one of my brilliant students," said Cas, also very surprised at how well she was speaking. "She's incredible."

"Wow, OK." said the father. "So, Sue, after the fight, the men from the other tribe came in and took the children," said the father.

"Yes, and they also took the pregnant women," she replied.

"How many pregnant women were there?" asked the father.

"Five, but at least one other was not showing so they didn't know about her," said Sue.

"What happened the next morning?" asked the father.

"When we went out in the morning, the one you call chief was standing there with five other Gorf men," said Sue. "They all had spears and had war paint on their faces."

"Were the Gorf men part of what happened during the night?" asked the father.

"It was dark, but I'm pretty sure they were not," said Sue.

"So what happened the next day?" asked the father.

"The next day there were three Gorf men in war paint guarding our village, and the day after that, just Chief," said Sue. "Can we give him that name?"

"Sure, from now on his name is Chief," said the father.

"Do you have a name other than dad or father?" asked Sue.

"Uh, actually, no," said the father.

"How about Joe?" asked Sue.

"Joe? Uh, OK," he replied, looking at Cas who just shrugged and nodded with a smile.

"Just so you know, Chief's job was to guard you women," said Joe.

41

"I know that, and he was a wonderful guard, Joe," said Sue.

"You should also know that the Gorf men intercepted the men from that other tribe and took our children and men to the Gorf village which is East of here," said Joe. "But there was no mention of the pregnant women."

"So, are the men and children safe?" asked Cas.

"Yes, and I think the Gorfs have been under seige by that other tribe ever since, so they haven't been able to bring them to us," said Joe.

"OK, so how can we get them back?" asked Sue.

"I'm thinking about going up there with Chief and taking along my rifle and Chief will take the shotgun," said Joe.

"Just you two?" asked Cas.

"If we encounter the other tribe, I think the guns will convince them not to try to stop us," said Joe.

"When are you going?" asked Cas.

"Tomorrow, first thing," said Joe. "Pat and you will have the other two guns. While we're gone, we'll have everyone stay in one location here and you two will guard them."

"We can do that," said Cas.

"And, obviously, everyone is coming along quite well with their learning," he said while pointing to Sue.

"Yes, with only a handful of somewhat slower women," said Cas. "And, as you saw the other day, we're almost finished getting them situated in the apartments.

"Some need a bit more training because their hygiene is not good enough yet," said Sue. Joe quickly turned to Cas, wide eyed, and smiled.

"Sue is now one of my helpers," said Cas. "She's an incredibly fast learner, and I've also started her and a number of others with

42

their education. I think that's obvious with Sue."

"It is," said Joe. "So, are you going to teach them everything that you and Pat have learned?"

"Of course, we're really just members of the same tribe so they're just like us and they need to know whatever we know," she shrugged.

"Very good," Joe agreed. "So once we get our men and children back, we can teach them too."

"And you're going up to the Gorf village to get them tomorrow?" asked Cas.

"Yes," said Joe.

"So we may see them tomorrow," said Sue.

"Well, if not tomorrow, as soon as we can escort them down here," said Joe.

"You fled here with Cas's mother a long time ago," said Sue. "So you were also attacked by this tribe?"

"That's a long time ago, so I don't think it was the same tribe, Sue," said Joe. "Our tribe was left alone for 20 years. This tribe also kidnapped our men and children and the other tribe just attacked. However, we weren't there after the attack so we really don't know what happened."

"I was a child at the time and I don't recall another attack or anything after until this latest attack where they kidnapped the children and men," said Sue.

"In my mind this current attack is by a completely different tribe," said Joe.

"I agree," said Sue.

"You never told us much about your experience back then," said Cas.

"Well, your mother and I were cuddling out in the bushes

43

when they came," said Joe.

"What did you do?" asked Cas.

"We got out of there," said Joe.

"And you eventually ended up here?" asked Sue.

"It was mostly crawling at first, slowly so we wouldn't be heard or seen," said Joe. "And I have always felt guilty for not helping the men defend the village."

"You wouldn't be here if you stayed to fight," said Sue.

"That's true dad," said Cas.

"I know, and at the time, with your mom to protect, all I could think about was getting as far away from the village as possible," said Joe.

"It was at night, so this could not have been easy," said Sue.

"That's right, it was dark with no moon," said Joe. "We crawled through the brush and grass until we could no longer hear the screams and shouting. Then we stood up and ran as fast as we could, stumbling and falling through the forest until we fell into the River. Then we flailed in the water until we somehow managed to get out. We eventually found the shallows and made it across where we collapsed and slept until dawn. The next day we were looking for a place to hide and saw a spot on the hill that seemed like a good place to hide. Behind a thicket of brush we pushed a few boulders aside and found a small opening. It took awhile, but we finally opened a large enough entrance to crawl inside where we spent the night. We lived there, foraging for food and sleeping there at night. Over the following days and weeks we found the vault and then the time capsule. The morning sun each day provided enough light for us to explore inside. It took a week or two before we were able to establish a hunting area to feed ourselves. In the meantime we explored the content of

44

the vault. It was filled with things we had never seen before. We also found the time capsule and were fascinated with it. It was designed for those who knew nothing, like us. So we began to learn how to use it. But it took a long time before we could read, and eventually talk. The little box that you crank spoke words and we just practiced speaking. All the while we kept an eye out for the other tribe that had attacked us, but they never came, and eventually we had Pat, and then you, Cas."

"Now you have us," said Sue.

"Yes, we now have the women of our tribe, and tomorrow we will go out to get the men and children of our tribe," said Joe. "We'll then be together, those of us who are left, and we must stay together at all cost." He made a fist and held it out front. Sue smiled and made the same fist and they touched fists.

Chapter 3

Early the next morning, Joe and Chief started up the valley to the East. The river wound a bit to the South as they continued, and it was several hours before Chief stopped to get his bearings. Ahead was where a creek entered the river. They left the river there and followed the creek for another hour before spotting smoke up ahead. It wasn't long before they were greeted by a half dozen Gorf men carrying spears, some had crude hatchets slung on their waste. As they approached, Chief let out a yell in a language that Joe did not understand, and It was returned by a chorus of similar shouts. Soon they were being greeted by the Gorf men who were curious about the guns that the two had brought. Once in the village, Chief told the men, and a few others who had gathered to meet them, about Joe's camp where the women from his tribe were housed, including Sue's apartments in that old building. By now, the men from Joe's tribe had joined the crowd, and he could see the children of his tribe being ushered into the square where they were meeting. Joe did not understand any of the Gorf conversation, and after more than a half hour of rapid chatter, Chief turned to him.

"The tribe has decided to move," said Chief.

"You mean to where we live now?" asked Joe.

"At first, yes," he replied.

"At first?" asked Joe.

"They're talking about relocating all the way to the coast," said Chief. "And I think it will be to everyone's benefit if your tribe moves to the coast with us."

"Well, actually, that's exactly what we've been planning to do," said Joe. "And with our new combined tribe, we will need a lot more hunting territory, so the coast makes a lot of sense."

"Yes, I agree," said Chief. "So they're going to pack up tonight and we can leave in the morning," said Chief.

"In the morning?" asked Joe.

"Yes, they've been wanting to move now for some time, so they've been preparing for it," said Chief. "Most everything is already packed."

"OK then, in the morning it is," said Joe.

The Gorf tribe had a little over one hundred people, and combined with sixteen men and a dozen children from Joe's tribe, it was a sizable migration that was stretched out for over a mile by the time it reached where the creek met the river. Joe was in the lead with his rifle, and Chief was in the rear with the shotgun. The middle was guarded with warriors sprinkled along the procession. They felt it was still possible for the other tribe to attempt an attack on them, so they were prepared, just in case.

Back at Joe's camp, Cas and Pat had been observing movement in the forest across the river all morning and by late morning they had concluded that it was not animals, but humans. The first thought that came to mind was the other tribe, and a possible attack. As a result, everyone moved into the apartments on the hill. Pat took up a position near the shallows with his 45, and Cas was guarding the entrance to the apartments with her snub nosed 38. But as she stood there she wondered if it would be more effective if both guns were there at the river, so she sent Sue down to ask Pat if she should come down. Sue picked up a steel rod that she found on the floor in the apartments and was partway down the hill when a large group of warriors suddenly burst from the forest and began rapidly charging toward the river. They were armed with spears and some had marked their faces with charcoal. As they grew closer to the river they began screaming unintelligible words while holding their spears high in the air. Pat drew his pistol and held it in both hands to steady his aim as they approached the shallows. He only had four bullets left and there were at least two dozen charging warriors, but he bravely stood his ground as he pulled back the hammer. Sue spotted the oncoming warriors as she ran, but instead of stopping or retreating, she began running faster, holding the steel rod over her head as if it would be a deterrent to two dozen angry warriors with spears, each warrior twice her size. The first of the shouting men entered the river as Pat prepared to shoot. He wanted to wait until they were closer so he could be certain not to miss his mark, which was their head. Meanwhile, Sue was nearly to the river as she now lowered the rod, pointing it at the men who were beginning to splash across the shallows. Suddenly, something powerful ripped through the lead two men sending them sprawling into the water with blood spewing everywhere. Their falling bodies tripped those immediately behind them, creating a pileup of bodies in the shallows. The remainder of the charging throng had stopped

48

cold behind the pileup in the river, their gaze now firmly fixed on Sue who had reached the river bank, still pointing her steel rod at them. The men were wide eyed, their mouths agape, as they stared at Sue in her bright orange outfit and steel rod pointing right at them. They suddenly began screaming, pointing at her. They dropped their spears as they turned to run as fast as they could back toward the forest. Some of those in the pileup had also seen Sue, and they got to their feet and followed the exodus toward the forest. In their wake were two bodies laying face down in the ripples and two others, struggling in agony from their wounds, trying to reach the far side of the river. As they struggled, one fell back into the river trying to get out, but one made it to shore and hobbled after the main group who were now almost to the forest. Pat was confused at what had just happened and turned to Sue.

"What happened?" he asked, mystified by what had struck the charging warriors and then why they seemed to run away in terror after staring at Sue.

"I don't know," said Sue, who noticed movement to her left and turned. Pat turned as well to see their father running toward them, carrying his rifle.

"I heard their screaming and ran ahead," he shouted as he drew near. "I was able to get off a shot."

"Wow, just in time, lucky for us," said Pat. "Sue was pointing that rod at them just as your bullet hit, and they ran like scared rabbits because I think they believed she was the one who made that happen."

"Ohh my god....really?" he gasped. Then they must have thought she's a witch or something. That's incredible since my rifle has a silencer and they wouldn't have heard it."

"The whole thing is amazing since Sue wasn't even supposed to be here at the river," said Pat.

"I know, but Cas sent me down to ask you if she should come down to the river so we'd have two guns here," said Sue. "But they charged out of the forest on my way down, and I wasn't about to stop."

"Right, you just kept coming down after you saw them charging," said Pat. "That took a lot of guts, so right now, you're definitely my hero!"

"Well, I thought I could at least hit one with this rod," said Sue, holding it up.

"You're a very brave woman, Sue," said Joe. "I think you're my hero too."

"We're just grateful that you showed up when you did, dad, or this would have turned our a whole lot different," said Pat.

"In any event, the end result might be to make them think Sue has superhuman powers, since I'm thinking that they probably already know about guns," said Joe.

"Well, they looked totally spooked as they turned and ran, screaming in horror," said Sue. "So maybe they do think I'm a witch."

"That's right, you might now be known as the Orange Witch of the Valley, Sue," said Joe.

"I'm not sure I like that name, but if it keeps them away, I'll wear it," said Sue.

It would be a few minutes before the first of the Gorfs arrived and the area began to fill. And it was the better part of an hour before Chief, who brought up the rear, arrived. Chief jointed Joe, Pat and Sue who were still standing near the river's edge staring at the three men in the river, two apparently dead and one still struggling on the other bank to climb out.

"What happened here?" asked Chief who had been nearly a mile away at the rear of the procession when the other tribe attacked, so he was completely unaware of what had happened.

"They attacked with at least–twenty five warriors," said Joe. "But I was able to get a shot off and dropped the lead warriors just as Sue was waving a steel rod at them. They ran off screaming. So we think they think she's a witch."

"A witch, OK, I'm not sure what a witch is, but if it keeps them away, it could definitely work to our advantage," said Chief, patting Sue on the shoulder.

"That's what we were thinking," said Joe.

"I'll have someone clean this up," said Chief, pointing at the two dead men.

"And maybe help that poor soul on the other side who seems to need some attention," said Sue. "We can take him in and care for him, and he might even want to stay with us."

"But he was just attacking us," said Joe.

"In your own words, Joe, he's just another human like us," said Sue.

"I hate it when my own words end up correcting me, but you're right, he is," said Joe. Sue just smiled and shrugged.

"I'll have him taken up to the camp," said Chief.

"Thank you…. so, based on what I see right now, I think we have to completely retool our plans for what we do next," said Sue, pointing to the newly arrived crowd. "We are now considerably bigger and if we want to stay together, I think we're going to have to make some major changes, including making that move to the coast we talked about, and making it soon."

"We're all on the same page regarding that, because Chief's tribe has that exact same idea," said Joe.

"OK, good," said Sue. "However, we need to sit down with our people and explain what we're planning, because this move is new to them," she said. "Keep in mind that we just moved all of us women into those nice apartments, which we love, and now we're telling them that we're moving, like, right away."

"I know, but this is a critically important move," said Joe.

"Of course it is, I know that, and I'll be the one that has to explain it to them," said Sue.

"You do that so well," said Joe.

"But I'm also one of those living happily in my new apartment," said Sue.

"Alright, I'll do it," said Joe.

"We'll do it together," said Sue who put her arm around him. Joe melted.

"Dad, I hate to interrupt, but you're absolutely not going to believe this," said Cas who was looking West down the river. From a big clump of trees a half mile away, a group of primitives were emerging.

"How can all of this be happening on the same day?" asked Joe, looking over at Sue who was still right beside him with her arm around him. She just shook her head.

"Right now, Joe, I'm wondering why someone isn't heading down there to greet these people?" Sue asked.

"Because I expected you to have already ordered that," said Joe. She elbowed him in the ribs, then started toward the approaching group. Joe tried to catch up.

"Pat!" shouted Joe over his shoulder. "I need you and Roy Rogers." Pat heard him and started quickly down from up on the hill. As he soon fell in behind his father and Sue he could see why his father had called him down.

"We've never had anyone arrive from that direction before," said Pat as he finally caught up with them.

"I know, that's in the direction of the ocean," said Joe.

"That's where we were talking about moving," said Pat.

"It's more than talk now, it's for real," said Joe.

"That's fine with me" he replied.

"We really have to move now with our expanded tribe," said Sue.

"I think it's the right thing to do, even though we have no idea what's down there," said Pat.

"If this tribe is from the coast, we'll soon know a lot more of what's down there," said Joe.

"Where else would they be coming from?" asked Pat.

"We'll soon know," said Sue.

As they grew closer it became more and more obvious that these were men and they were dressed in skins like most of the tribes in the area, but the fact that they all carried spears did not lessen the possibility of a confrontation, which was why Joe had summoned Pat to join them. Once the tribe was close enough to see each individual clearly, their voices could be heard, and it sounded like familiar words. Sue counted them and there were ten in the group. They had not moved since they saw them coming. When they were less than fifty feet away Sue held up her hand to signal for them to stop.

"Is that English we hear?" asked Sue who of course was first to speak.

"Yes, and you too," said one of the men.

"Well, your arrival is quite coincidental because we have recently had a significant expansion to our tribe and have decided to move to the coast, which is likely where you're from," said Sue.

"And while we didn't expect anyone else to show up today, the fact that you did somehow seems appropriate."

"Yes, we are from the coast," said the man. "So just how soon were you planning to move there?"

"As soon as we can get our shit together," said Sue.

"So what's going on here anyway?" asked the man, pointing to the large gathering up ahead. "Has there been a major event of some sort?"

"Well, yes, there was quite an event not long ago," said Sue. "You see, we've had some serious problems with another tribe, and we are just getting some of our people back. They had been kidnapped by this other tribe. And just as they were arriving back with us, this nasty tribe launched an all out attack on us. Fortunately, we were able to repel it and they retreated into the forest." She pointed to the South at the forest.

"Holy crap, you have had quite a day, haven't you?" asked the man as those behind him began chatting among themselves after hearing Sue's account.

"Yes we have, and a third tribe that is here right now are the ones who were able to get our kidnapped members back for us," said Joe, pointing to the congregation behind him.

"Another tribe got your kidnapped people back?" asked the man.

"They did, and they're going to move to the coast with us," said Joe.

"And then this nasty tribe attacked you here this afternoon?" asked the man.

"That's right," said Sue. "It was the same tribe that kidnapped our men and children, and killed our elderly."

"Killed your elderly?" asked the man.

"That's right," said Sue.

"What did they want with your men and children?" asked the man.

"They want to teach them to believe whatever it is that they believe," said Sue.

"So what about the women of your tribe?" asked the man.

"Well, they would have taken us too if it wasn't for the Gorfs.... again," said Sue.

"Again?" he asked.

"They also intercepted the nasty tribe and took our kidnapped men and children from them," said Sue.

"You call them the Gorfs?" asked the man.

"It's a tribe of larger, hairier humans that look different than us but are in every way, just us," said Sue.

"I think I know about this tribe," said the man. "I didn't know what their name was or anything about them, but I've heard about them."

"They're wonderful people, and we love them," said Sue.

"I would too if they did what you say," said the man.

"Now we consider them essentially part of our tribe," said Sue.

"And they're part of that congregation up there?" he asked , pointing.

"They are," said Joe.

"OK, so what's with the gun?" asked the man. "We've never seen a gun before except in books. Where did you get it?"

"It's a long story, but if it wasn't for these guns we might not even be here now," said Joe.

"I see, but you said guns, in plural," said the man.

"We have four, but with very limited ammo," said Joe.

"I want to here more about the guns, but right now, I'm also interested in knowing about the clothes you're wearing, and the hair cuts," said the man, pointing at Sue, then Joe and Pat. "You're beginning to look like what one might consider civilized people," said the man.

"We're just like you with clothes and a haircut," said Sue. "But let's sit down back there in the grass and talk about that and a lot of other things. You must have been walking for quite some time."

"Yes, sitting down sounds good to me," said the man.

"But first, I'm Sue, this is Joe, and that's Pat with the pistol, impersonating Roy Rogers."

"Pleased to meet you," said the man. "I'm Jack and these are my fellow tribal members from down on the beach."

"We're pleased to meet all of you," said Sue reaching out to shake Jack's hand. A round of introductions followed. She then pointed to a grassy area part way up the hill and waved them to follow her. A few minutes later they were all sitting in a big circle on the hillside.

"So what brings you all the way up here?" asked Joe.

"We just relocated from another site along the ocean and had not had the chance to check out what was in the upland area," said Jack.

"Why did you move?" asked Sue.

"Mostly because another tribe kept starting fights with us and we had lost several of our tribe in those fights," said Jack.

"That sounds like what we've been dealing with," said Joe.

"You mean the tribe that kidnapped your people?" asked Jack.

"Yes," said Sue.

"It does sound like it could be the same tribe, but it's a long way from here to the beach, so perhaps it's another tribe with similar ambitions," said Jack.

56

"That may well be, and what a coincidence that you show up here at this very moment with a similar problem," said Sue. "According to the Gorfs, this other tribe is trying to convert other tribes into their way of thinking," said Sue.

"What do you mean, convert?" asked Jack.

"Teach others whatever they believe," said Joe.

"So they kidnap your men and children, and kill your elderly?" asked Jack.

"A bit extreme don't you think?" asked Sue.

"A bit," said Jack.

"And, as we said, just a little while ago a large band of them launched an attack on us right here," said Sue.

"But you managed to fend them off," said Jack. "With the guns I assume?"

"Yes, I did shoot a couple of them, and Sue did an impression of a witch that freaked them out," said Joe.

"Wait a minute....a witch?" asked Jack.

"It's true, I swear," said Joe. "We buried two of them and we took one that was wounded in as one of our own."

"So you shot them with that pistol?" asked Jack, looking at Pat.

"No, I have a rifle with a scope and silencer," said Joe.

"You have what?....A rifle with a scope?....and a silencer? And Sue here is impersonating a witch?..... boy, this is some story," said Jack.

"I know, and the day isn't even over yet," said Sue.

"However, just to qualify the gun issue, we have only a few bullets left for each gun, and when the ammo is gone, that protection ends," said Joe.

"I understand that, but maybe you need to start at the

beginning and let us know how you arrived at this point in time," said Jack.

"Sure," said Joe.

"First of all, how did you get the guns?" asked Jack.

"I'll give you the short version," said Joe. "About twenty years ago, I and my deceased woman came here to this location and found a time capsule and a sealed vault. The vault had all kinds of useful items, including several guns and fabric to make clothes and a lot of other things that have helped us become more civilized. The main thing the vault and time capsule had was the materials needed to teach us how to read, and then speak."

"That's interesting, because my ancestors also found a time capsule but it only taught them how to read and speak," said Jack. "Our ancestors then taught us how to read and speak. Over the years we have been able to find a wealth of things along the beach, but no guns or other things to make us more civilized."

"We're not sure why, but they left a few bullets for each gun, except the rifle that I use for hunting. The rifle was left with more shells and that seems to have beeen done that way for a reason, likely something to do with it's value to us for hunting food."

"I guess I never really thought about that before regarding guns," said Jack. "I only thought how nice it would have been to have one. So now I'm not quite as jealous as I was when I first saw Pat's pistol."

"So tell us more about you and your tribe," said Joe.

"Yes, you said you just moved to a new place on the beach," said Sue.

"OK, well, we're just getting settled there," he replied.

"And you moved because a tribe similar to our nasty tribe had been attacking you," said Sue.

"That's right, and we're still a bit concerned that this other tribe will just show up again in our new location," said Jack.

"Based on our experience, that's entirely possible," said Joe.

"We have to move because our hunting ground is no longer within easy reach, and of course because we have no idea when this other tribe will attack us again," said Sue.

"So, for both of us, it's either run or fight, and we're a small tribe that's aging, so we chose to run," said Jack.

"Well, we're not a small tribe anymore, and we have the Gorfs in our tribe now," said Sue. The Gorfs are clearly better able to battle the nasty tribe, but even they are wary of them after they saw some of the warriors of the nasty tribe with large knives, which is something they do not have," said Joe. "Neither do we."

"Yes, the tribe we're dealing with also has knives," said Jack. "That's why we don't want to fight them."

"We still have an advantage over knives with guns, but when the bullets run out, they'll get that advantage back," said Joe.

"So I guess the big question involves whether there is room for another tribe on the beach?" asked Sue.

"The beach goes on for miles and there's plenty of fish, seafood, seals and sea lions for meat and coats," said Jack. "Plus, if you are our neighbors and have guns, that's an advantage that we do not presently have."

"Then you need us," said Sue.

"I guess we do, but since there's plenty of room on the beach you would still be welcome, even if you didn't have guns," said Jack.

"Thank you," said Sue.

"Because of the necessity to protect our hunting area, you may have to locate a ways away from us," said Jack.

"No problem, we assumed that," said Joe.

"As we said, we were planning to move right away," said Sue.

"You mean like tomorrow?" asked Jack.

"No, we'll need a few days to get everyone and everything ready for such a move with so many people," said Sue. "And the fact that our tribe is essentially dug in means we'll have to uproot our people."

"I suppose we can wait here with you for a day or two so we can show you the way and arrive at the same time," said Jack.

"I was just going to ask if we could do that," said Joe.

"It will be quite a surprise to your tribe, since they'll only be looking for you to return," said Sue.

"Surprise is an understatement," said Jack.

"The fact that you and your tribe have already lived there on the beach and determined what you need to live there makes it that much easier for us to move to a strange place where we would otherwise have no idea what to prepare for," said Sue.

"That would have been our biggest challenge because it's so entirely different than living where we do now," said Joe.

"Actually, we need to make sure everyone is aware that we're moving right away, since many of them are only aware that it's in the talking stage," said Sue.

"Right, we need to get on that," said Joe. "So we're going to have to leave you Jack, but we'll be back."

"That's fine, I understand," said Jack.

"OK, I'll tell the women, like we agreed," said Sue, who took Joe's hand.

"And while you're doing that I can go over this with Chief and he can inform the Gorf tribe, even though they're essentially ready now," said Joe, who was again entirely melted as the two of them walked off toward the crowd.

"I'll let all of our new people know what's going on," said Pat to Sue and Joe's back as he realized they were completely preoccupied with themselves.

"Oh, and if we could, after you notify everyone of your plan, I would like to know more about this place!" said Jack, almost shouting after the two.

"Maybe after dinner!" shouted Sue over her shoulder. Jack just smiled as he watched them walk away hand in hand.

After the entire congregation had eaten and had separated into little groups, Joe, Sue, Jack and some of his men went up to the entrance to their bunker and sat in a circle in the grass.

"One of the big adjustments for us was dealing with odors," said Sue.

"Oh yes, odors, but you learn to just live with it," said Jack. "It's difficult to do anything else when you have just one piece of clothing and it's an animal skin."

"Lucky for us, because the vault that Joe found had a good supply of fabric and sewing materials," said Sue. "So Joe, and particularly his daughter Cas, began making clothing for themselves. They also used the scissors they found in the vault to cut their hair. Joe even found a razor to shave his face. But it took a bunch of women to design some of the more fancy clothing you see in the crowd. And now that we have a whole new tribe to integrate into our way of living, we have a lot more work to do on a whole range of issues as we creep in the direction of being civilized."

"You're way ahead of us on that front, but we look forward to getting help catching up," said Jack. "We still walk around in animal skins and long hair."

"You said your ancestors found a time capsule like ours and it provided you with the same or similar teaching module that taught

61

you how to read and speak, so that's a real plus," said Joe.

"Yes it is, but we're still just a village of long haired, smelly primitives speaking like civilized people but looking like savages," said Jack.

"I know Jack, but you have the ocean, so you can wash your faces, underarms and private parts everyday, or as often as you can. Every one of us does it every day in the river," said Sue.

"We could bathe I suppose, but then we have to go back and put on our trusty sealskins," said Jack. "Plus, if you dunk yourself in the ocean, it leaves some of it on your skin and when it dries it can be uncomfortable for some of us, especially the women."

"Don't you have any fresh water to rinse off with?" asked Sue.

"Well, your river flows onto the beach near us, so we have that, and the little lake it makes before it ends up in the ocean," said Jack. "But the lake is our water supply, not our bathtub."

"Alright, so take a dunk in the ocean, and then rinse off where the fresh water meets the ocean so you don't foul the drinking water," said Sue.

"I guess we could," said Jack with a shrug. "But I'd like for you to convince our women, because in terms of odor, I think they may out stink our men."

"You're right about that, and I'd love to do that," said Sue.

"She would," Joe nodded.

"I also think we might also have enough fabric for you to build some decent clothes for yourselves," said Sue. "And scissors to cut that hair back a bit."

"You'll have to teach us all of that," said Jack.

"No problem," said Sue. "And another thing with women, they have periods once a month."

"Oh, right, you mean the blood?" he asked.

"Yes, so we found a large supply of some things you put where the blood comes out, and it absorbs it," said Sue. "Then you put them in your poop hole because you don't want to have your yard filled with bloody sticks."

"Would you have enough of those for our women?" he asked, shrugging as he smiled at Joe who just shrugged back.

"Well, yes, but the supply will run out before too long," said Sue. "However, now that we get the idea behind it, we can probably make something like it."

"So you might also have a few things that we can use," said Joe.

"I'm sure we do, especially since you've never been to the coast and have never fished or lived on the beach," said Jack.

"Exactly, we're beach virgins," said Joe.

"Yes, but until our two tribes meet, we'll have to see how everyone gets along before we start assuming everything is just peachy," said Sue.

"Where did you find her?" asked Jack. "She's like the Wizard of Oz that I read in fairy tale books."

"She's read every book in our library including the Wizard of Oz," said Joe.

"Well, so far she's like a waterfall of good ideas and wisdom," said Jack.

"I just listen to her for what to do," said Joe.

"And she's such a beautiful woman too," said Jack.

"I'm already taken," said Sue, pointing to Joe.

"Oh, I've known that from when we first met," said Jack. "And I think everyone who has seen you two together knows it."

"Is it that obvious?" asked Sue.

"It is and it's not a bad thing, it's a terrific thing, because my

Susie and I are like that too," said Jack. "And by the way, speaking of baths, where do you bathe since there aren't many bushes near the river? You don't bathe naked do you?"

"Of course we do," said Sue. "If we're all naked at the same time, nobody needs to have privacy. Besides, naked is how we came into the world."

"I know, but people in our tribe don't like to be seen naked," said Jack.

"Actually, we were like that too before we came here, and never used to bathe at all, but now we're all used to it," said Sue. "However, we do like to poop and pee in private."

"So you just strip off and get into the water?" asked Jack.

"Well, we need to get clean all over and you can't do it with your clothes on," said Sue. "When there are no hotels or bath houses like the olden days you bathe in the nude. This is not Waikiki."

"What's Waikiki?" asked Jack.

"In one of her books," Joe shrugged.

"So you think my tribe should bathe in the nude in the ocean?" asked Jack.

"Well, you can't bathe in a sealskin, and if you want to deal with the odors, you're going to have to clean up and clean up daily," said Sue. "We also have bars of soap that have a nice smell, and the women love them. So we can supply you with a couple of bars."

"I'm not sure how this will go over with our women, but I definitely hear you regarding odors," said Jack.

"Oh, I think once they see us frolicking in the surf in our birthday suits, I'm sure they'll want to join in," said Sue.

"Birthday suits?" asked Jack.

"In the books," said Joe. "And you realize that she's read and pretty much memorized the entire English dictionary," said Joe.

"The dictionary? What? We have one and I can't believe anyone would even consider reading it, let alone memorizing it," said Jack.

"The thing is, she reads almost as fast as she can turn pages," said Joe.

"Now I'm sure she's the Wizard and I also understand why you say, 'what she says'," said Jack.

"So I have a question Sue, do you have any idea why this other tribe is so intent on spreading whatever they believe in to other tribes?" asked Jack.

"OK, so first of all, our time capsule did not teach us one of the hundreds of ideologies or religions that existed in the distant past, so we were only given books of what is called settled science, basic knowledge and history," said Sue. "A child must be taught an ideology, you are not born with it. We, as primitives, are in effect like children. And remember, there were hundreds of ideas on how to live, and many ideologies and religions. So in order for this other tribe to have learned whatever they learned, it must have been included in their time capsule, or someone came here and taught it to them."

"OK, I agree with that," said Jack.

"So then, assuming they were taught an ideology or some belief, it must be something they have been taught to believe in very strongly, suggesting it could well involve life and death, possibly an afterlife," said Sue. "Secondly, in order to defend their belief from those who don't believe in it, they seem to want to get everyone else to believe as they believe. That way there is no opposition to it."

"But if it's for them personally, why are they trying to push this idea on others?" asked Jack. "Is it just to have everyone believe as they believe?

"I don't know, and I especially don't know why their belief is so intense, but I assume it has something to do with the thought that it is so wonderful that everyone else needs to have what they have, even if they have to go to extremes to spread their joy," said Sue. "Or, it could be more sinister than that, which is something I suspect, but as I said, I really don't know."

"What they're doing is not exactly the best way to share something so wonderful if that's what they think it is," said Joe.

"They are taught that it is, and have not been taught any alternative to it, so they have no way of comparing it to anything," said Sue. "But I think those who are most aggressive and use forceful tactics like kidnapping are a minority in the tribe. Of course the entire tribe gets painted with their belief, whatever evil they end up doing."

"And some end up dying, like those today, even though they may be just part of the movement, not the leaders or the more dedicated?" asked Jack.

"That's right, but let's say that if each tribe believes intently that only their idea is the most wonderful, and others make the same claim that theirs is the most wonderful, the friction that results can reach a fever pitch as history has shown," said Sue. "Wars have been fought, and the big war had a lot to do with this friction among beliefs."

"In other words as a human race we're killing and dying over whose wonderful is the best wonderful?" asked Jack.

"Well, yes, I suppose, even though it's a lot more complicated than that." said Sue.

"So, it's not what the books say about the ideologies or religions is it?" asked Jack.

"No, of course not," said Sue. "It's about different ways

66

of living, and any ideas that clash with other ideas that are the opposite often result in serious fighting. To me, it just doesn't seem possible that the only super intelligent animal in the world could actually try to destroy its own species over what are, to a complete outsider, petty forms of disagreement."

"Doesn't that also describe how each side seriously felt that they alone were the ones who sought peace and were therefore the innocent ones?" asked Jack.

"Yes, righteousness has no faults," said Sue. "And it ultimately stems from the fear that if you argue against another's ideas, you are arguing against everyone associated with that idea, even though a majority on both sides might be quite amenable to compromise or backing away. And if it reaches the ultimate point of believing that suicide is worth it to defend the idea, or the idea of its leader, there can be no limit to how far it can go. At that point, nobody is safe. Because if they also believe in an afterlife, death is just a passage into another, better, life, so the fear of dying is no longer an impediment in their effort to eradicate their enemy and defend their belief."

"So are we now, today, many thousands of years after the big war, repeating the same song?" asked Jack.

"I hope not, but it does seem to be looking that way," said Sue. "Look, surviving in the wild is difficult enough without having to fight among ourselves while we are trying to survive."

"Well, all that being said, the question remains, where do we go from here to keep this conflict with these tribes from consuming us?" asked Jack.

"Well, as I watched what was happening today, it was clear to me that this attack was not staged by every one of those in that group," said Sue. "It was organized and led by a few, possibly even a single individual, whom I think is now dead. While I'm not ready to let our guard down, I feel that this threat is lessened without that leader. But history tells us that for every leader that falls, another rises to take their place. You can kill people, but you can't kill their ideas. If history is repeated, the fact that our guns will run out of bullets and no longer protect us, will require us to continue running away, or else figure out how to end these other tribes' ambitions."

"I totally agree, but, again, where does that leave us?" asked Jack. "We moved to where we are on the beach, but what if they keep coming after us, do we keep moving?"

"I think for now, while we still have bullets, let's just continue doing what we were planning to do and not let this incident stop us," said Sue.

"OK, so let's start preparing for a move to the beach," said Joe.

Chapter 4

"Ohhh, I see what you mean about a lot of space," said Joe, as they arrived at the cliff above the beach and saw the panorama with sand and driftwood stretching out in both directions, and the sea disappearing forever into the haze. They had been strung out for over a mile as they trekked much of the day, carrying their possessions and stopping on occasion for a rest.

"Our tribe is there on the left, this side of the waterfall," said Jack.

"Then the waterfall is our river flowing over the cliff," said Sue. "And there's that nice pond of fresh water that you mentioned, near where it empties into the ocean."

"Right," said Jack who now saw a group from his tribe directly below them and they had begun to wave. He waved back. Sue and Joe joined in.

"How nice, a greeting party," said Sue.

"And that's my woman, Susie starting up the trail," said Jack excitedly, as he started out ahead of them.

"Of course they're not expecting an entire village to show up, so we have a bit of explaining to do," said Joe.

"Little do they know they're about to be invaded," said Sue.

"I'll see you below," said Jack over his shoulder, as he pulled ahead quickly down the trail.

"Wait for us," said Joe.

"No way," he replied as he continued down. Sue and Joe tried to keep up but were losing ground. Joe stopped a moment to wave for the others to follow. Before long, the path that wove its way down the steep embankment to the beach was lined with their tribe.

"Who are all these people?" asked Susie, after she and Jack had met and hugged.

"Another tribe that decided to move down here," said Jack.

"Move down here? Where are they going to….." she began.

"Don't worry…..down the beach," said Jack. "They're not moving in right next to us."

"Wait, what?" asked Susie as Sue walked up to them all neatly dressed in clothes with short hair and shiny face. Sue had her arms open for a hug, and Susie, not sure what to do, finally decided to accept the hug.

"You're just like pictures from the past that I saw in books.," said Susie while Sue was still hugging her.

"I know I don't look like I fit in with your tribe, but I'm from a tribe that looked exactly like yours a little over six months ago," said Sue who now stepped back at arms length. "And, actually, some of them you will soon meet still do."

"But you talk like us," said Susie.

"Look, we had material to make clothes and scissors to cut the hair, so we did it," said Sue.

"I want to look like you," said Susie, now getting excited.

"Well, we have soap to make us smell nice, material for clothes, and a lot of other girly things," said Sue.

"Oh god, I love it, and now we'll be neighbors," said Susie.

"Obviously the women are going to be key to how our two tribes get along," said Jack.

"Without a doubt," said Joe.

It would be more than an hour before the entire tribe was able to make its way to the level area before reaching the driftwood littered beach. By now Jack had already spoken briefly with a number of his tribe about what was happening. They had been literally shocked to see him arrive with a new tribe, especially one so large. And the fact that some were dressed in clothes was something they had only seen in books. Though perhaps the biggest surprise were the Gorfs, which was a tribe that they had heard about but never seen. There seemed to be a mixed reaction to the Gorfs moving in, and it took a brief speech from Sue, standing on a piece of driftwood to explain to them that they were just a larger and hairier version of themselves. As the newly arrived tribe began to settle among the plentiful driftwood just down the beach from Jack's tribe; Jack, Susie, Joe and Sue sat together near the water to talk things over.

"We actually have no idea what was in the stash from our time capsule since we didn't find it ourselves," said Jack. "In fact it was hundreds of years ago that it was found, but I'm pretty sure it didn't have anything like what was in your vault. We did get a small store of books that came with the learning module."

"Well, the learning module that taught your ancestors how to read and speak was the most important gift of all," said Joe.

"I agree," said Jack. "It awakened us to a whole new world that we otherwise would have lived the rest of our lives without knowing about."

"I know, our books were like a key that opened the door to the vast wealth of knowledge that humans had accumulated over the centuries, from their awakening long long ago, to the great war that could have ended it all," said Sue. "While we don't know the full extent of what happened in that war, it could have closed that door to the knowledge and technology that was responsible for creating the modern world that took so very long to create."

"And now, since that door is still open, we at least have the possibility of rebuilding that knowledge base, and even the technology," said Susie. "But we need a lot more books."

"I know, a lot more books, as well as other educational materials," said Sue. "That recorded knowledge is the heritage of the human race, and we're at the very beginning. It's a quest to recover our extended brain."

"Extended brain?" asked Jack.

"A clever name for the sum of all the accumulated knowledge of the human race," said Sue. "Without it, we're just like we were before we found our time capsule, savages wandering around in deer skins with long hair."

"Seal skins and long hair," said Susie.

"The books are the first step," said Sue. "But recreating the technology will be an incredibly long journey, since it took so many so long to develop what we once had," said Sue.

"I know, and I wonder if we will ever get back to where we were as a world society before the war?" asked Jack.

"I don't know, and since we don't have a clear history of what has happened since the war, or even how long it has been since the war, we have to assume that progress could have been made elsewhere if there were survivors whose cities and homes were not destroyed," said Sue. "We might even be surprised to find out that there are areas like that where they have progressed to unimaginable heights."

"I think that's entirely possible," said Joe. "It's a very big world."

"We really don't know, but hopefully some day we may find out," said Sue.

"Based on our world, I think we can assume that a lot of other areas like ours were entirely wiped out during the war," said Jack.

"True, but we are completely ignorant of what has happened elsewhere, so we just have to take what we're given and make the best of it," said Sue.

"That's right, so what we have is what we have," said Susie.

"And since we're at the very beginning, progress for us has been very slow. My ancestors, after finding the time capsule, figured out how to make a number of basic items, like paper, so we know how to make that. It's great for wiping your butt. But the capsule didn't leave us any directions for how to make cloth like you found in your vault."

"Paper to wipe our butts is a lot better than what we're now using," said Sue."

"What were you using?" asked Susie.

"You don't want to know," said Joe. "But we did get a much better supply of things in our vault to deal with other everyday issues."

"Including Kotex," said Sue.

"What's that?" asked Susie.

"Women have periods once a month," said Sue.

"Oh I know, and?" asked Susie.

73

"You stick this thing up your you know where to soak up the blood," said Sue.

"Oh, right, so you don't bleed all over," said Susie.

"Then just throw it in the poop hole," said Sue.

"I want those," said Susie.

"I think we have enough for awhile, but with so many women now, our supply won't last that long," said Sue.

"And you said you have more fabric like you used to make your outfit," said Susie.

"We do, and like I said before, if we didn't have that fabric, we'd be wearing what you're wearing," said Sue. "Look, I can ask our women to fit your women and men with clothes. So how many of you are there?"

"About eighty, I think," said Jack.

"Oh, that's a lot of outfits, so it might take awhile," said Sue. "We also have to fit the Gorf tribe, and as a result this may be something we'll have to ration."

"I hope we can, because I am so jealous of your clothes right now," said Susie.

"We'll have a lot to share now that we're neighbors," said Sue.

"I think we have two challenges at the moment," said Joe. "One is to combine the talent and resources that we agree to share with one another, and two is food, and how we can hunt in the vicinity of one another and still supply our people with enough to eat."

"That second challenge will have a lot to do with where you locate your tribe," said Jack.

"And keep in mind that some in our tribe are a little uncomfortable with the Gorfs," said Susie.

"I understand, they are clearly different in appearance and

have a different language, but they are so nice," said Sue. "These people saved our children and our men that were being kidnapped by that other tribe. And Chief has been the protector of the women of my tribe. He is, in every way, one of us, and so are the rest of the Gorf tribe."

"I know, but I suspect that racial prejudice is not a thing of the past and we may still have to deal with it here," said Susie.

"I've actually thought about that possibility," said Joe. "So we'll locate the Gorfs on the other side of our tribe for now. And just looking at what's out there, I think it may actually be around that bend in the beach, so they might even be out of sight."

"Thank you for that, Joe, and just so you know, Jack and I feel the same as you do about the Gorfs now that we've had a chance to meet them and hear from you about your experiences with them," said Susie. But it may take some time to get the rest of our tribe to accept them as if they're one of us."

"Eventually we'll make this work, I'm sure of it," said Sue.

As they were sitting there, Joe turned to look down the beach at the cliffs. Some of the hills directly in front of the cliffs had a shape that made him think. They were clearly not entirely natural in shape, and he thought they may actually be buildings that existed before the war. Jack saw him staring at the hill.

"Odd looking hills aren't they?" asked Joe.

"Yes, and after we saw your apartments, I'm wondering if there might be buildings under there too?" asked Jack.

"That's exactly what I was thinking," said Joe.

"Or, considering where it is located, my guess is that this might actually be a ship," said Sue.

"How would a ship have ended up against the cliff like that?" asked Jack.

"The sea level has risen and fallen over the centuries, and tsunamies from earthquakes occur on occasion, so it could have easily washed up there," said Sue.

"How do you know all these things?" asked Jack.

"She reads a lot," said Joe.

"Alright, so let's say it could be a ship," said Jack.

"I think it could because of it's shape," said Sue. "I would guess that it might even be a cruise ship like those I've seen in books."

"I don't know what a cruise ship is or looks like," said Jack. "We have books, but we don't have the extensive library that you have."

"Well, from what I've read, a cruise ship is a ship with thousands of cabins that would take people around the ocean just for fun," said Sue.

"Thousands of cabins?" asked Susie. "And people live in them while they're out on the ocean?"

"They live in them in luxury," said Sue. "These ships were like entire cities on the water."

"If it is a cruise ship, then it went aground before the big war, right?" asked Jack.

"Not necessarily, because the big war may have happened far earlier than we think, and if there were survivors from that who had the technology and resources to build something like this, then they did," said Sue.

"That's entirely possible since we have no idea exactly when the war took place, or if there were survivors of that war with the eventual ability to do something like this," said Joe.

"Well, if it is a cruise ship, and if we were able to dig it out, we could live in those cabins," said Susie.

"Of course," said Joe. "We were living in the rooms of a

building that we partially uncovered back where we lived," said Joe.

"Then we have to start digging," said Susie.

"Well, we may have to do a few other things before we start on that," said Jack.

"Why?" asked Susie. "This could be home to one or both of our tribes."

"I know, but uncovering that thing is a massive job that could take a long time," said Jack. "It's covered with a lot of dirt and we don't have a lot of things to dig with."

"Look, the Egyptians built the great pyramids long before modern machinery," said Sue.

"What are the pyramids and who are the Egyptians?" asked Jack.

"Never mind, if we want to dig it out, we can dig it out," said Sue.

"Remember?" asked Joe.

"I know, 'what she says'," he replied.

"I happen to agree with her," said Susie. "You men are so doubtful of what us women can do."

"Not me," said Joe. Sue hugged him tightly and he put his arm around her.

"I do think we have a lot of important things to do first," said Sue. "So we may have to attend to those before tackling a project like this."

"I know," said Susie. "Such as moving in, which is no easy job, and building me some clothes like you have."

"I can start on that tonight," said Sue. "Let's see, I think we're about the same size."

"Susie has bigger, uh…." Jack began.

"Tits," said Sue. "Every woman in every tribe has bigger ones than me."

"I like them just the way they are," said Joe.

"I know that," said Sue "So I'll put a little more material in certain places because I also think your hips are a bit wider than mine."

"I like them the way they are," said Jack.

"You two stay out of this," said Sue.

"Jack, let's go talk about guns, hunting and stuff like that," said Joe.

"Yes, I want to know more about that rifle with the silencer and scope," said Jack. "You have to show me how that works."

The two of them wandered off by themselves.

"You could pick off someone way up there on the cliff," said Jack, as he fondled the rifle that Joe let him hold.

"That's true, but remember, this rifle is strictly for hunting because I have only a few more bullets," said Joe. "The rifle sunsets when it no longer has bullets. It's then no more than a fancy club."

"And that's the case with all of your guns since you have only a few bullets for each of them," said Jack.

"Yes, and that's why I'm trying to think past where we are right now," said Joe. "That includes what we talked about just now with Sue and Susie."

"Oh, right, the cruise ship," said Jack. "You're thinking we might have to move again, so perhaps we might not want to do that at all?"

"We need to think ahead, not just for now," said Joe.

"I know, especially the day when we no longer have guns," said Jack.

"Yes, and with so many unknowns, it's nearly impossible to plan that far ahead," said Joe. "We need to keep the future in mind as we go about settling here, or settling anywhere."

"Have you discussed that with Sue?" he asked.

"She already understands the situation we're in," said Joe. "But I'm afraid I've fallen head over heals in love with that woman, and I don't want to upset her by pressing this concern too hard."

"Actually, Joe, I've only known her for a short time, but if you want to share something with this woman, just do it," said Jack.

"I know you're right, but I don't want to place any stress on her." he replied.

"Joe, for her, the stress would be for you having the stress, not her," said Jack.

"Yeah, I suppose you're right, knowing Sue," said Joe.

"So let's sit down with her and Susie and talk about how critical we think our situation is," said Jack. "Susie is very smart too, and I know I don't appreciate her nearly enough. Look, if we put our collective heads together, we can come up with some options for how to extend our vision of the future to more than just digging up cruise ships."

"You're right Jack, I'm glad I was able to share this with you because it's been worrying me a lot lately," said Joe.

"It's getting late, so let's sit down with them tomorrow and go over this, and try to come up with some options," said Jack.

The next morning, the four of them sat together on what was becoming their piece of driftwood, overlooking the ocean.

"We really haven't spoken much about the future because of all that's going on right now," said Joe.

"Is this about what you mentioned to me last night before we went to sleep?" asked Sue.

"Yes, the question of what happens when we run out of bullets," said Joe.

79

"And that has to do with this other tribe, and whether they are still a threat to us here in our new home," said Sue.

"Yes, because if we're faced with a serious threat from this other tribe, we can't just go out and get help from another tribe," said Joe. "We're really on our own, and that includes all of us, which is really three tribes. We're all really on our own."

"Joe wants to share with you two what he has in the sack he has on the ground next to him," said Sue.

"You have something?" asked Jack. "Something from your vault?"

"Yes, it's from the vault," said Joe.

"Something that can help us with that threat from this other tribe?" asked Jack.

"Well, possibly, but I don't know," said Joe. "It's some kind of signaling device that you would use if you needed help."

"What kind of signaling device?" asked Jack.

"I'm not sure what it does, but apparently it sends out some kind of electronic signal," said Joe.

"You said it doesn't have any information about who we might be signaling to," said Sue.

"No, there was nothing that came with the device about that," said Joe. "It only indicated that it was there to use if you needed help."

"Ever since you mentioned it to me, I've wondered why they would even leave such a device, not knowing when their time capsule would be found, or whether anyone would be out there to receive such a signal at an unknown future date," said Sue.

"My thoughts exactly," said Joe. "But at this point I'm not sure what other options there are for seeking help, if indeed we want to get help."

"I for one think we do," said Susie. "But I agree with you about no one out there to receive it, and then, if they did, who are they and will they actually come here."

"And whether they will help us or harm us," said Jack.

"On the other hand, if someone left a time capsule, wouldn't they also know that the survivors who found it might need help at some point?" asked Sue. "It would be in an unknown future, and they would have no idea who would have survived with enough capacity to help whomever found the capsule. But human nature suggests that people help people. Maybe those who left the time capsule had a little faith in human nature. Everyone out there is not trying to take advantage of others. People do help people."

"Very well put, Sue," said Susie. "I like your interpretation. I think it makes a lot of sense."

"Maybe they knew there were survivors out there that could respond based on any need we might have for assistance," said Sue.

"I like that interpretation too," said Susie.

"So do I," said Jack. "And, of course, there may be no one out there at all to receive the signal. Of course, we have no idea who is out there today capable of receiving it, or what they might do if they did receive it."

"I love Sue's take on this, and feel that we really don't have a lot of other options right now for seeking help," said Joe.

"It's like an SOS that I read about," said Sue.

"SOS?" asked Jack.

"Save Our Ship, which was a distress signal sent by a ship that was in trouble, asking for help from anyone who could hear their cry," said Sue.

"This device only offers the option to send a signal, it doesn't describe what the problem is or anything about why we're sending it," said Joe.

"That's like the SOS that I read about, except it's just a buzz or a tweet or some sound, that's it," said Sue.

"Look, if there are survivors out there with superior technology, maybe one of them is within hearing distance and will hear our beep or tweet and wonder why it's coming from what is known as a wilderness," said Susie.

"Very good, Susie, that's it," said Sue. "A signal from primitives. Any technically capable person should realize how odd that is and respond."

"From where?" asked Jack.

"What's out there on the horizon?" asked Sue.

"You can see fuzzy forms of what look like islands out there," Jack pointed.

"Or maybe someone in a boat could also be out there," said Sue.

"Well, I think it's a long shot, but maybe someone is out there," said Joe. "Who knows who might respond, since we know virtually nothing about what's out there."

"Including how incredibly advanced they might turn out to be," said Sue.

"And that might be a good thing, not a bad thing," said Joe.

"They might also know that time capsules were left for these primitives, and SOS signaling devices were included in those capsules," said Sue.

"Why do I always believe that you're right?" asked Susie.

"Because she usually is," said Joe.

"Look, I believe we're overthinking this," said Sue. "We should just send the damned signal and see what happens."

"What she says," said Joe.

"So you're sending it?" asked Jack.

"I have it right here in my bag," said Joe who reached down and pulled out a small oblong box with a crank on one side.

"So you just turn that crank and it sends the SOS," said Sue.

"Well, first I go to the highest hill and hold this thing over my head, then turn the crank until I hear a whirring sound, and continue cranking for a few minutes," said Joe.

"Highest hill?" asked Sue. "Wait. Actually, I think the beach here is fine because from where we used to live, and where the capsule was found, a hill would provide a clear view of the horizon. But here on the coast we have a clear view of the horizon."

"What she says," said Jack.

"I know," said Joe who held the little box over his head and turned the crank, faster and faster until it began to whir. He kept cranking for a few minutes.

"That's a small generator that produces a current to activate the radio signal," said Sue.

"Of course it is," said Joe shrugging as he smiled at her.

"Now I guess we just wait," said Jack.

"Until something happens," said Susie.

"Actually, I'll be amazed if this results in any kind of response considering when the device was placed in the capsule and the limited range of such a signal," said Sue.

"Which means, we need to just go on with what we were doing," said Joe. "First and foremost is to start planning for when we don't have our guns and nobody has come to our assistance."

"No, despite the odds, we must always have hope," said Sue. "I'll be very surprised if anyone responds, but I'll continue to have hope, at least for the rest of the day."

"You're right, because you never know," said Joe who now

took her hand.

It was several hours later at mid afternoon, with everyone busy getting ready to move down the beach to the new village, when Chief, the ever vigilant guardian of the tribes, who was patrolling along the area above the beach, stopped and was looking toward the ocean. He stared for a moment, and then began to shout.

"Everyone to their stations!" He yelled. Those who could hear him turned to find where he was before reacting. They saw him pointing out to sea, and all eyes within hearing distance turned and began scanning the horizon. In the distance, sticking up a couple dozen feet above water was a black tower plowing toward them. Everyone waited patiently as the tower moved closer. As it approached, the water parted around the tower as it began to surface. When it was a few hundred feet offshore, it came to a stop. By now, Joe and Sue had joined Chief who had come down to the beach directly in front of the strange ship. Sue decided to wave, which resulted in a blinking green light at the top of the tower. Sue then motioned for whoever could see her in the ship to come ashore. They waited.

"What is it?" asked Jack, his mouth agape.

"It's a submarine," said Sue. "An extremely large one."

"I don't know what a submarine is, but it's clearly some kind of ship that sails under water, right?" asked Jack. "At least they picked a deep area in the water where they can get close."

"You're right, it does, but it seems a lot bigger than those I've seen in books, and it would need deep water to get this close I would think," said Sue.

"Well, it's definitely huge," said Joe. "And apparently it received our signal for help."

"Apparently," said Sue. "It only took a few hours to get here, so it couldn't have been that far away."

"What do we do, just wait for someone to come out?" asked Jack.

"That's all we can do," said Sue. "I doubt seriously if whoever this is has anything to do with what those who placed our time capsule had in mind, so we might want to be a little cautious about what we do next."

"Right, we have no idea whether this is friend or foe," said Jack.

"Well, what we do know is it's someone who received our signal," said Sue. "So let's wait for someone to come out of this tub and find out who they are and what they want."

"Speaking of which," said Joe as a woman dressed in a black skintight outfit emerged from an oblong hatch in the tower, followed by six other women in identical outfits.

"I certainly love what they're wearing," said Susie.

"I know, I want one," said Sue. "But maybe what we have to talk with them about is slightly more important than acquiring one of their outfits."

"I'm not sure about that, but yes, I think we need to at least talk with these women first before we ask them where they got their outfits," Susie said while smiling at Sue who just shrugged.

"Of course, so let me see if they're friendly first before we start celebrating our good fortune at having someone respond to our SOS," said Sue.

"That's right, because I think this might be a serious encounter since they seem to be in uniform," said Joe.

"Let's not speculate, let's just greet them and go from there," said Sue who stepped forward and began waving. The first woman, who had a red collar on her suit, waved back.

"You received our signal!" Sue shouted through cupped hands.

"You speak English," said the woman into the mic in her hand. The sound was both loud and clear.

"Of course, doesn't everyone!" shouted Sue. "I like your outfits!"

"Thank you," said the woman. "My name is Jo."

"I'm Sue, this is Joe, Jack and Susie!" she shouted, pointing to each as she said their names.

"And these are?" asked Jo waving her hand over the entire beach that was now crowded with most of Sue's village and some of Jack and Susie's. The Gorfs were off to one side.

"Don't be misled by what you see!" shouted Sue. "They are all like us except for clothes and a haircut!"

"OK, so you sent the distress signal," said Jo, as if that was something they usually received.

"Well, there's this other tribe upland who may look like us but are not nice and friendly like us. In fact, they're downright vicious!" shouted Sue.

"You do seem nice, and you've educated yourselves," said Jo.

"You seem nice too, so why don't you come ashore so we can discuss this whole thing without me having to yell!" shouted Sue.

"Roger, give me a minute," said Jo who motioned to her crew and someone ducked inside to retrieve a bag that they threw into the water. When it hit it expanded into a raft. Another crew member retrieved oars, and threw them in while Jo was descending to the raft on a ladder that had been deployed from the side of the sub. A few minutes later, Jo was sliding up onto the beach and Jack and Joe grabbed the handles on the raft and pulled it farther up onto the beach. Jo stepped out and Sue was right there with her arms open for a hug. Jo hesitated a moment but then smiled as she

86

hugged Sue. Susie was right there for her hug, and Joe and Jack wrapped their arms around everyone.

"We had no idea who would respond, or what would happen if we sent the SOS," said Sue after they let Jo off the hug.

"You're from tribes that found a device in your time capsule," said Jo.

"We are," said Sue. "Susie is and Jack's tribe also found a time capsule, but apparently no signaling device, and you obviously know about them."

"We do, and we're alert for those who signal us," said Jo.

"Which is why you were not that far away when you heard this one," said Sue.

"Yes, this is an area we patrol," said Jo.

"Joe found the time capsule about twenty years ago, and he and his woman learned how to read and speak," said Sue. "They then passed what they had learned on to their two children and eventually to us. A little over six months ago most of us were primitives who couldn't read or speak anything intelligible. We were primitives. So, even though we can converse with you now, we know only what was in the library of books that was in a vault that contained the time capsule. We know absolutely nothing about the current state of affairs in other parts of the world."

"You did exactly what those who left the vault and capsule intended," said Jo. "And it looks like it's still a work in progress." As she spoke, Jo was looking around at the hundreds of people, some of whom were clothed like Sue but many were still in animal skins.

"We clearly have a ways to go, and at the moment our situation is uncertain because of this other tribe that seems to want to convert us to whatever it is they believe," said Sue. "We actually fear for our lives. Although we have a few guns that were supplied in the vault, we have only a few bullets left, so we're not sure what to do after that."

"Actually, that's why we're here," said Jo.

"You mean you know about this other tribe?" asked Sue.

"Of course, that's our job," said Jo.

"Your job?" asked Sue. "You mean you will do something about them?"

"We don't, but we report their location, and someone will come here and clean this up," said Jo.

"Clean this up, as in what?" asked Sue.

"Eliminate this other tribe," said Jo.

"You mean kill them?" asked Sue.

"We don't get into how they eliminate them, but the tribe will no longer be here to cause you any more trouble," said Jo.

"I and my woman escaped an attack by another tribe some twenty years ago, and for some reason that other tribe never caused trouble again, so I'm wondering if your outfit also eliminated that tribe?" asked Joe.

"Most likely," said Jo. "But that was before I was on this route, so I'm not sure how they were notified."

"I was just wondering, and now I know," said Joe.

"You seem like you're in the military because of your uniforms, and the fact that you arrived in what seems to be a piece of military hardware," said Sue.

"We are what I would loosely define as military, and yes, this submarine is a piece of military hardware," said Jo.

"So your mission is to eradicate these troublesome tribes?" asked Sue.

"Yes, that's pretty much what we do," said Jo.

"Tribes that try to convert other tribes to their belief by forceful

88

and often deadly means?" said Sue.

"Yes," said Jo.

"Well, we're not sure what they teach, or whether they pray, or who they worship, so we have no idea what they want to convert us to," said Sue. "But they kidnapped our men, our children and our pregnant women, and killed our elderly."

"That's a good description of those tribes," said Jo.

"And then you refer them to someone else for elimination," said Sue.

"Yes, that's our job," said Jo.

"OK, but one very important thing, Jo, I'm fairly certain that everyone in this type of tribe is not entirely committed to whatever they believe, and therefore they are not really criminals as such," said Sue. "From the behavior that I've observed, I've concluded that it doesn't take much for any one of them to essentially drop out of what they're doing and become one of us."

"So you think many in that tribe are really innocent, and it's just the leaders and active followers that need to be eradicated?" asked Jo.

"I feel certain of it," said Sue. "This is true especially the women and children, but also, many of the men. And I have plenty of witnesses and an actual outlaw tribe member here today to prove it."

"You know what Sue, I know you're absolutely correct about that," said Jo. "And I've known it for many years, but have never done anything about it, and to be honest, I feel quite guilty about that," she replied, a tear forming in the corner of her eye.

"Well, as you said, you're just doing your job, Jo, like a good soldier," said Sue.

"That's been my excuse for not saying or doing anything about it," said Jo.

"Look, you just report what you find to others who do the actual extermination," said Sue.

"And then innocent people are included in the extermination, so why am I innocent if I know that what I have done is wrong," said Jo.

"That's because in your heart, you're a kind and caring person," said Sue, reaching over and putting her arm around her. Jo now had a tear running down her cheek.

"I do want out, but I'm just not sure what I could do to get out," said Jo, holding back a sob.

"Well, actually, I think you can get out," said Sue.

"I can?" she asked.

"Yes, and at the same time, help us get out," said Sue.

"How?" asked Jo.

"I'll tell you, but first, I would like to know more about the rationale behind this type of action," said Sue. "First of all, do you know how this came about? I mean how did the people you work for identify this belief that they want to stamp out?"

"I'm not sure entirely, but I think the rationale seems to be that this type of belief, and others like it, were one of the main causes of the great war, and so it's important to stop it before it can spread to more people," said Jo.

"I see," said Sue. "So what is it about this type of belief that makes it so dangerous?"

"I'm afraid I've never been told, just that it was an important activity to ban from the planet, along with weapons of mass destruction," said Jo.

"It seems to me that this belief might fall into the same category as one of the peaceful religions of the past," said Sue.

"I suppose it could, but I don't think these tribes would be considered peaceful under any definition," said Jo.

"That's right, so, if someone practices a peaceful religion, they cannot get painted with the same paint as those who use their belief to promote their type of violence?" asked Sue.

"No, I think with this belief, they are willing to basically commit suicide to defend or promote their belief," said Jo. "For them it's just a transition into a wonderful afterlife, and not really suicide in their minds. But unfortunately, the suicide can be for a dictator or strong leader instead of a transition into an afterlife."

"OK, so then it's all about this afterlife?" asked Sue.

"Right, they believe that they are not really dying, but simply transitioning into the peace and tranquility of a life after death," said Jo.

"But you think some actually go into battle and lay down their one and only life for their leader, with no afterlife?" asked Sue.

"Apparently, but like I said, I don't really know for sure," said Jo.

"Whatever the case, if the fear of dying is reduced or eliminated, the outcome can be catastrophic in the context of a war," said Sue. "And so it's assumed that this was a contributing factor that led us into the big war. So I guess I can see the rationale for stamping it out, if that's the case. I just don't think what they're doing to stamp it out is either humane or effective, since the belief is still there no matter how many believers you eliminate."

"I'm sure you're right, Sue, but they just keep stamping them out," said Jo. "So why do I continue referring all these people to certain death?"

"I understand your frustration, and appreciate your feelings about your role in it," said Sue.

91

"So, did your society, that promotes this policy of extermination, survive the war with much of their technology intact?" asked Joe.

"Yes we did, and today our society lives in cities that are so incredibly different from what was there before the war that it literally defies my ability to describe them to you," said Jo.

"Incredible, and of course we had no idea anywhere like that even existed," said Sue. "Here, we are thrilled to find fabric for clothes or Kotex for our periods." Jo held her hand over her mouth to hold back laughter.

"She's right, we have been living off the land like our primitive ancestors for our entire lives, until now," said Susie. "Sue and Joe had a vault with their time capsule, and it was filled with some basic necessities for realizing a more civilized life, including guns."

"You do realize that guns have been banned forever, and the penalty for having one is death," said Jo.

"Oh wow, but without them we might have been dead anyway," said Sue.

"Well, our guns sunset when the bullets are gone, which is likely to be soon, so maybe it doesn't really matter that we have them," said Joe.

"So don't tell anyone we have them," said Sue holding her finger over her mouth. Jo smiled and did the same.

"But do you have any weapons at all?" asked Jack.

"We have some," said Jo, pulling out a small pad that fit in her hand. "This will entirely stun a person and leave them nearly helpless for hours."

"But it doesn't kill them," said Sue.

"No," she replied. "The ban of course also includes nuclear weapons and anything that can carry weapons in the air."

"So, no airplanes, satellites or missiles," said Sue.

"That's correct," she nodded.

"Is your society worldwide?" asked Sue.

"No, the world is divided into a number of societies," said Jo. "Ours covers much of former countries that front the Pacific Ocean. But the bans on weapons is worldwide. We don't have regular communication with the other societies so we really don't know what they enforce, believe or do."

"I don't understand, how is it possible for these bans to be enforced?" asked Sue. "I can't see how enforcement by individual societies would hold up over time. There has to be some kind of world-wide control that includes weapons necessary to enforce the bans, or it would simply evaporate into chaos and the kind of face to face conflict that occurred leading up to the big war."

"You're right Sue, and there is such an organization," said Jo. "But I am sworn not to discuss it with anyone."

"Does the general population in your society know of its existence?" asked Sue.

"In general, yes, they do, but those with a need to know are the only ones who can get involved in the direct interface between the world organization and each of the particular societies," said Jo.

"And I, of course, don't have a need to know," said Sue.

"You don't," said Jo.

"OK, so let me speculate, and without saying anything, you can nod if I'm right, or shake your head if I'm wrong," said Sue.

"I'm not sure if that's permitted, but nobody will know since I'm basically sitting in the wilderness with no one watching," said Jo.

"OK, so let me speculate," said Sue. "We don't see any satellites or airplanes?" asked Sue. Jo nodded.

93

"What about geosynchronous satellites at undetectable altitudes distributed around the globe so that all surface areas are being viewed at all times. Is that possible?" asked Sue. Jo nodded.

"Since you have no weapons in the Pacific to exterminate anyone, is it possible for this worldwide control organization to be behind the extermination of these evil tribes that you refer for extermination?" asked Sue. Jo nodded.

"If this worldwide organization has existed for thousands of years, isn't it unlikely that humans could continuously staff and manage it without becoming humans that fall completely off the rails at some point as humans are likely to do?" asked Sue. Jo looked at her and hesitated, before she nodded.

"So, what if humans were assisted by robots, which would likely be necessary anyway because of the enormous amount of surveillance data they would have to monitor 24-7, and then act upon." said Sue. Jo again hesitated a moment again before nodding.

"And over time, don't you think that the robots would find the humans both unreliable and dishonest, and they would have to completely take over the operation in order to make absolutely certain that there were no violations in the global rules to avoid another war?" asked Sue. Jo was now smiling and shaking her head, but then she nodded. She then walked over to Sue and hugged her.

"Where did you come from?" asked Jo.

"Jo, we're like children," said Sue. "Give us the information, without prejudice and politics, and we see through what's going on better than someone who grows up with all of the biases and influences that have been installed into our learning as a civilized society."

"I think you're right about most of it, because too much happens that we have no control over, and robots and artificial intelligence is very much a part of human existence in today's world," said Jo. "Could the robots just take over? Probably. Did they? I'm sure you're right, they did. But I would amend your assumptions by suggesting that it was a human decision to turn over the enforcement of the ban to the robots. As you correctly described, the complexity and sheer size of the job is just beyond human capabilities to implement on a 24/7 schedule. They are essentially watching every corner of the entire surface of the planet every second of the day and night."

"This is something that is almost inconceivable to our feeble human minds," said Sue. "So does this organization have a name?"

"Just The WO," said Jo.

"And to complicate it further, the remaining humans have divided up the world into dozens of little fiefdoms where they have applied their own versions of how to live in a war-free world," said Sue.

"Fiefdoms," said Jo with a little laugh. "That's right on, actually. Good description."

"So. In the case of the American continent and the African continent, for example, they have two sides, each side with a different society," said Sue.

"Yes, but in the case of North America, it has been kept as essentially primitive from shore to shore since there were so few surviving urban complexes," said Jo. "The areas that were considered wilderness covered most of the land area. Of course I'm not certain about the Eastern Shore, it might have resettled under Atlantic jurisdiction."

"This was the only continent wiped so clean by the devastation?" asked Sue.

"Oh no, vast areas of Asia are now in that category too," said

Jo.

"Why North America?" asked Sue.

"I think it had too many enemies after it became withdrawn from the rest of the world," she replied.

"So it had no friends?" asked Sue.

"Oh no, it had it's friends, but it did not help defend them, so they didn't help defend it," said Jo.

"OK, so it was just left to remain primitive," said Sue. "And apparently someone came here from somewhere to teach a belief to the primitives that had evolved in the wilderness. And your little fiefdom wants to rid the world of those people, with the assistance of the WO?"

"No I think WO is more than just an assistant, I think they may even be behind the policy," said Jo. "But I'm not sure."

"Well, because if they do the extermination, they have some role, but I wonder if it's in support of the Pacific policy to off these tribes, or if it's to just move them somewhere that will not affect those tribes like ours," said Sue. "In other words, their version of extermination may well be a relocation to another area where the tribes there are of the same belief."

"Oh my god, I actually think you're right, because it would be the right thing to do and would be consistent with the establishment and maintenance of a peaceful world," said Jo.

"I think it's the most likely scenario," said Sue.

"My god, how do you know all of this, Sue," said Jo.

"It just makes sense," said Sue. "So, do you know anything about the Atlantic Ocean societies which are on the other side of America?" asked Sue.

"No, just rumors," said Jo.

"Like what?" asked Sue.

"That they tends to segregate races, beliefs and just about everything else," said Jo.

"That sounds virtually impossible, but then dividing the world into countless fiefdoms, each with their own rules for living, can result in just about anything I suppose," said Sue. "And it would explain where the WO relocates our evil tribes. To Eastern America where they are segregated."

"Again, what you assume makes sense," said Jo. "And yes, it makes sense that the Eastern part, while it could still be primitive, would be controlled by the Atlantic policies."

"I'm just wondering if there are any societies out there that we could live in without the kinds of policies and rules like here in the Pacific," said Sue.

"Well, actually, without these aggressive tribes, you could live here safely," said Jo.

"I ask you Jo, would you live here if you had a free choice to move elsewhere?" asked Sue.

"No, probably not, now that you put it that way," said Jo.

"We are essentially in a wilderness, and yes, we could stay here, but now that we know what is out there in the rest of the world, I think we would want to go out there and seek our place in it," said Sue.

"You mean, take advantage of the modern benefits and lifestyle," said Jo.

"Exactly," said Sue.

"I know I would, and I think it would not take even a moment of convincing to get everyone on this beach to want that," said Susie.

"I wonder if there are any in-between areas, or areas open to all ideas and beliefs?" asked Sue.

"Maybe, but you'd have to check that out in person to find out," said Jo.

"So why don't we take a trip and do just that, check it out in person?" asked Sue.

"Wait, you mean in my sub?" asked Jo.

"No, I thought we'd walk," said Sue. Jo reached out and pushed Sue on the shoulder while laughing.

"You mean you four and me?" asked Jo.

"No I mean everyone on this beach, your crew and you," said Sue. "The whole shooting match."

"Everyone, oh.....how many of you are here?" asked Jo.

"Maybe four hundred," said Sue. "And they all are easily trainable to use a modern toilet, have been thoroughly coached in hygiene, and we can even get many of them dressed in clothes, with hair cuts, so they almost look civilized."

"Well, I have a few hundred uniforms in the sub, and the sub is actually designed to hold up to five hundred, but there are only a little over three hundred separate births," said Jo.

"A number of us will double up," said Sue.

"What about food?" asked Joe.

"We have stores for over a year, but that's for a maximum of thirty crew, so we're talking about maybe a month at most with everyone here," said Jo. "And the food is not restaurant quality."

"I've only seen pictures of a restaurant, but we're used to knocking off a seal or two for dinner so I doubt if anyone will complain," said Sue.

"I love this woman," said Jo.

"So do I," said Joe. Everyone laughed.

"Look, we have characterized Sue as the Wizard of OZ, like in the childrens book," said Susie. "So why don't we make this a search for the Emerald City, where we can all find what we are looking for.""The Wizard of Oz, I think I vaguely remember that," said Jo.

"So then are we ready to follow the yellow brick road, Jo?" asked Sue.

"The yellow brick road, uh, OK, but I'll be AWOL, so I'll have to make the initial call on where we go first, which is the hell out of the Pacific," said Jo.

"No, problem, that's your call," said Sue. "One question: do you think the WO will be interested in tracking us since they will obviously have the ability to do that."

"If I stay on my usual route for awhile, they may not notice," said Jo. "And if we travel deep we shouldn't be detected unless they get suspicious and activate their deep sea scan capabilities," said Jo. "And besides, I tend to cruise far and wide on my route, so the first leg of our trip to the tip of South America shouldn't be too unusual."

"But since they are, I assume, watching us, and will see us load four hundred into that sub, then take off, it might suggest something unusual," said Sue.

"I've transported prisoners and troops from place to place in the past," said Jo. "That's why the sub is so big and can carry so many."

"But what happens when we head into another ocean?" asked Sue.

"Unusual, yes, but I see nothing that suggests a violation of the WO ban on war-like activities," said Jo.

"And it's worth the risk," said Sue. "So, we have a lot of work to do to get this crowd of primitive-looking people starting to look presentable and trained to live in a tin tube."

"Shall we say a week from now for departure?" asked Jo.

"I think we can do it sooner if we try," said Sue.

"So let's get going!" Sue shouted, after having turned around to shout to the tribe. Some had heard their discussion and knew what she was talking about. They cheered. The rest had no idea what was being discussed, but most of them cheered anyway.

It would be nearly a week before they were ready. Uniforms from the submarine were distributed and fabric from Joe's vault was used to finish clothing for those who did not receive a uniform. Most of the latter were Gorf men who would not fit into the uniforms. Many Gorfs were still unable to speak English, so a school had been established on the beach. Hygiene would be important on a submarine, so lessons in the correct use of toilets, cleanliness, tooth care and other sanitary necessities were conducted daily. By the time they were ready to leave, everyone had some training in every essential they would need in the compact spaces of a submarine. It still left more education and training for the trip. But it wasn't known exactly how long the trip would take, nor where they were going to end up. The symbolic destination of the Emerald City was the imaginary destination where they could realize their dream of being in a happy place where they could live in peace. The six leaders, Sue, Jo, Joe, Jack, Susie and Chief sat together on the beach the night before they were to leave.

"I think we're ready," said Sue. "We will still have to have daily lessons on a number of things, so perhaps by the time we get to our somewhere, we should be well on the way to becoming civilized."

"It's remarkable what you've done so far," said Jo. "When I came here, many of those I saw looked like those from a primitive tribe, but now it almost looks like a gathering in one of my ultra modern cities."

100

"Under the smell, the long hair and animal skins were people just like any other human here on this planet," said Sue. "We have a long way to go with education, but that will come with time and more reading materials."

"So, I guess we can begin loading first thing in the morning," said Jo. "That will likely take a few hours for everyone to get in and get settled before departure."

"We'll use the catamaran that we built out of driftwood for fishing to ferry people to the sub," said Jack.

"Good, because that rubber raft would never work," said Jo.

"Then we just follow the yellow brick road," said Sue.

"I've never sailed into a fairy tale, but I like the idea, since we're all looking for a place that can help us find what we need in our lives," said Jo.

"I sense that most of our people are excited and ready for an adventure," said Sue. "Unlike you, Jo, none of us have ever even seen anything modern, let alone dreamed of riding in anything as exciting as your sub, so this will be something very special, and the fact that you showed up when you did is a fairy tale in and of itself is special. I can't even begin to tell you how grateful I am, and I'm sure every single person in our tribe feels the same about what we are going to do. So thank you, Jo."

"Look Sue, when I received your signal and came here, I had no idea this would be something that would completely change my life," said Jo. "And it is a change in my life for something I had only dreamed of. I never liked this job and never believed in what I was doing. Once I discovered what it was, I actually thought it was evil. But then I met you and Joe and Jack and Susie, and really, everyone in your tribe, I knew right away what my true calling was. So I think we both have a lot to be thankful

101

for, and, I believe that I'm the lucky one. You are helping me live my life's dream. Thank you." She leaned over and hugged Sue, and again tears ran down her face.

Chapter 5

"Welcome aboard the ship everyone," said Jo, from her seat in the conning tower next to Sue and one of her crew. She and Sue were being seen by everyone on dozens of screens throughout the submarine. She then looked at Sue, who would speak next.

"This will be new for all of us since we have never seen anything like what we're riding in," said Sue. "We're not even sure where we came from or how we got here since there is no written record of us after the war wiped out our part of the world. What we know is what has been passed down from generation to generation among our primitive ancestors living in the wilderness. That was mostly hunting skills and ways to avoid being eaten by other animals. But that is about to change in a big way. For the next days and weeks we will be living in tight quarters, so we will get to know each other in ways entirely new to us. Because we are living like this, in close quarters, it is critically important for us to practice good hygiene and good manners. For those who understand what I'm telling you, please find some way to communicate this to others who do not yet speak English very well. I know we have gone over this many times this past week, but now it is time to practice it. Don't be a stinky neighbor. Use the bathroom. Take your shower at least two or three times a week and use soap when you do. Brush your teeth at least once a day. We have plenty of fresh water on the ship, but your showers are timed out at one minute, so you'll have to soap up and wash quickly. Don't end up all soapy. If you decide you have to have sex, do it out of sight in complete privacy, even if it's just the standard twelve second dip. Jo says we will try to stop to go out on land to walk around when we can. We will try to wash our clothes every week if we can, and everyone must do it. There are shows and entertainment on your screens, whenever you turn them on. There are also games in the game areas and crew to show you how to play. Please contact someone if you are sick, injured or need to ask a question. Someone is here to help. Now, sit back and enjoy our adventure."

"Very good madame stewardess," said Jo, after turning off the broadcast. "So just exactly what is a standard twelve second dip?"

"All animals, of which humans are one, are assumed by nature to be a product of nature and the natural environment," said Sue.

"OK," said Jo, shrugging.

"So in the wild, as nature has assumed animals live, copulation is for reproduction," said Sue.

"And?" asked Jo.

"Copulation is carried out efficiently, and therefore quickly, and for humans that act is programmed by nature to last about twelve seconds," said Sue.

"So men are programmed to complete sex in twelve seconds?"

asked Jo.

"Apparently," said Sue. "I just repeat things, I don't make them up."

"OK, well that explains a lot," said Jo, shaking her head with a smile and raised eyebrows.

"I'm just hoping that wherever we end up will have people who will be willing to accept this collection of recovering primitives," said Sue.

"I wouldn't worry about them fitting in, because wherever we end up will likely have other races of humans as well as others whose immediate ancestors were reduced to primitive status after the war," said Jo.

"So, you're thinking it will likely be a populated area rather than something like a deserted island?" asked Sue.

"Yes, an area that is populated will offer us the best chance for long term survival," said Jo.

"I guess that's right," said Sue. "We were in a primal world searching for food, and we don't want to just locate in another primal world still searching for food," said Sue.

"Exactly," said Jo. "I'm hoping we can find a place similar to where I used to live, where survivors of the big war were able to advance in science and convenience in ways that will seem almost unimaginable to you and your tribe."

"I can't wait to find such a place," said Sue. "As long as it doesn't impose unrealistic rules for how I live my life."

"Of course," said Jo. "And oh, I'm sorry we couldn't take your horses, but obviously we couldn't have taken them."

"I know, but they'll survive on their own even though Joe's two children are disappointed."

"The other thing I need to emphasize is the fact that me, my crew and this sub must locate well outside of our zone of influence," said Jo. "That means out of the Pacific."

"No, we won't want to stay in your zone either, so not to worry," said Sue. "Does your society have any capabilities to either monitor other areas, or initiate a chase in other areas?" asked Sue.

"Just the WO, and that organization oversees all areas, so even though they cooperate with the authorities in this zone, they should have no interest in getting into local operations unless they involve issues related to the ban on war type activities or actions that might lead to compromises in their ability to keep the world from sliding into another war," said Jo. "I don't think what we're doing crosses into their areas of concern."

"I can't imagine how it could, but of course we'll just have to see," said Sue.

"Even though my crew and I will also be guilty of AWOL and stealing this sub, what we're doing should be considered local business as far as the WO is concerned," said Jo.

"And the fact that we're sailing south within your normal route, it should also be considered just routine patrol," said Sue.

"I have a great deal of flexibility in my searches, so I don't think going south will raise any immediate concern, not even with my own authority," said Jo. "And we'll be traveling deep to avoid detection from most of their equipment."

"Then let's travel deep," said Sue.

"We just need to be entirely out of the Pacific as quickly as possible," said Jo.

"But will you be considered the enemy if you show up in another Ocean?" asked Sue.

"I don't know, but I can't imagine why I would," said Jo. "I think our problem in other oceans is the fact that we will be

106

strangers in a submarine." said Jo.

"Meaning we'll have to keep our heads down as much as possible," said Sue.

"Of couse we'll have to surface from time to time," said Jo.

"I know, otherwise we'll never know where we'll meet a friendly face," said Sue.

"I also don't know if the two ocean societies consider each other enemies, or have rules barring visitors from other societies," said Jo. "I just know what our society does, and they definitely stop and question anyone coming into the ocean from elsewhere."

"What do they do after they stop them?" asked Sue. "Ask them to sign a pledge to follow the rules of your society?"

"I think the main questions are how long are they staying, what is their business, and when did they plan to leave," said Jo.

"Do they then keep track of their whereabouts?" asked Sue.

"They do, but some visitors are always disappearing, so I'm not sure how effective their surviellance is," said Jo.

"It sounds like the immigration process is at least somewhat loosely administered, and I hope that's the case in other oceans," said Sue.

"We'll just have to see, and as we do, exercise extreme caution," said Jo.

"We just have to avoid being taken into custody by anyone," said Sue.

"Yes, above all else," said Jo. "One of the complications we might face is the fact that these two ocean societies are not countries, but rather organizations of like-minded leaders."

"True, but that shouldn't change what they stand for and what they do," said Sue.

"That's generally true, but attitudes and how rules are applied might change depending on where you are in the ocean," said Jo.

"Over thousands of years, I wonder how many different iterations of what they do now has changed before it reached what it is today?" asked Sue.

"I have no idea, and it will likely continue to change in the future," said Jo.

"I think change is inevitable, and the longer the time frame, the greater the change" said Sue. "Humans evolve, not just physically, but mentally and politically. That's more reason why the WO was formed and had to be turned over to machines that do not evolve or change in their ultimate purpose."

"Well, our ocean changed leadership and policy many times in the past, and I'm sure it will change many times again in the future, but it is what it is now, and I'm not waiting for it to change again," said Jo.

"I agree, I want something differeent," said Sue. "Our life spans are now."

"That's right," said Jo. "So we have a number of different ocean societies with different behavioral objectives, but thanks to the WO, they possess no massively destructive weapons to defend their beliefs."

"Our basin does have these stun devices, and our ships have tractor beams that can disable another craft, but that's it," said Jo.

"So, as we travel in this sub, we know they have what you call a tractor beam to disable us, if they can get close enough," said Sue.

"Yes, but if we travel deep I think we'll be safe from that," said Jo.

"Alright, I like deep," said Sue.

"But of course when we do come up, we can be detected and disabled," she replied.

"So my next question is, how far do we have to go before we can no longer be detected by your ocean society?" asked Sue.

"I don't think I would feel safe until I rounded the tip of South America," said Jo. "And then, on the other side, we also must run deep because we have no idea what capabilities the other side has for detecting a sub."

"How far is it to the tip of South America?" asked Sue.

"About 7,000 miles," said Jo.

"How fast can this sub travel underwater?" asked Sue.

"It would vary a little depending on ocean currents, but about fifty miles an hour," said Jo.

"So, let's see, about a week to get there?" asked Sue.

"You did that in your head?" asked Jo.

"Simple math," said Sue.

"I might be able to cut that to six days and change," said Jo.

"Could we make it three and three with one stop in between?" asked Sue.

"That would risk being spotted," said Jo. "But if we stop near a known stop of ours, they might think I'm on an official visit."

"I think we should risk it considering we're traveling with cruise virgins who have never done anything remotely similar to this," said Sue.

"Well, we could stop in the Galapagos, which is one of our ports," said Jo.

"So have you stopped there before?" asked Sue.

"No, my beat is more in the northern part of the Americas, but I understand that other subs stop there," said Jo.

"Alright then, just follow the yellow brick road, and we'll see what we see," said Sue pointing South. Jo looked at her with a smile, then went to her controls to get the sub in motion.

A few days later Jo announced they were approaching the Galapagos Islands where they would surface for a day and have a chance to walk around a little. But as they drew near with just the tower above water, they saw that several ships were docked near where she had hoped to stay. While still assessing what to do next, a fast moving boat came steaming toward them. As she picked up the mic to announce they were departing there was a loud thunk and she looked at Sue and Joe who were there beside her.

"What?" asked Joe.

"They slapped a tractor on us," said Jo.

"I think this requires quick action," said Sue. "Joe, get your rifle,"

"Wait, what are you thinking?" asked Jo.

"Shoot the bastards," said Sue.

"Shoot? Oh but, I'm not…..," said Jo.

"Look, call them and tell them you're on official business and to release the tractor," said Sue. Jo hesitated a moment, but finally clicked the dial on the radio and picked up the mic.

"We're here on a call," said Jo into the mic. "Why the tractor?"

"We didn't know," came the reply from the small ship that had now stopped not far away.

"So release the tractor," said Jo, after waiting a few seconds.

"We have to wait for verification," came the reply. About that time, Joe appeared with his rifle.

"We can't go out on deck since we're not surfaced, so is it possible for Joe to climb up that ladder and peek out?" asked Sue.

"Well, there's an escape hatch up there, but….." said Jo.

"I'm heading up the ladder," said Joe.

"Uhhh, OK….crap…..when you get there, just hit the emergency button and wait," said Jo hesitatingly.

"Got it," said Joe who disappeared up the ladder.

"What's he going to do?" asked Jo.

"Do you have an emergency tractor beam release or something?" asked Sue.

"You mean can I override the tractor in an emergency?" asked Jo.

"Can you do that?" asked Sue.

"Yes, but that would be seen as hostile and they would immediately reactivate a secondary, handheld, tractor, and that one cannot be overridden," said Jo.

"Alright, so we just have to do what we can," said Sue. "So tell one of your crew to be ready to override the tractor."

"I hope you know what you're doing," said Jo who signaled to one of her crew who was near the tractor override switch.

"You do not have authorization!" said someone over the speaker.

"And look, he has the secondary tractor in his arms, in case we try to override," said Jo looking at the screen.

"Joe, are you at the hatch?" asked Sue.

"Yes, ready to go out," said Joe.

"Alright, go outside very slowly, then quickly shoot the device that's in a man's arms on that ship. Try to hit just the thing in his arms, and not him, with one shot," said Sue.

Joe hit the emergency hatch button and peeked out. He spotted the man, put the device in the crosshairs and fired. The device flew from the man's arms, spewing sparks. The impact sent the man back, hard against the bulkhead. He bounced forward off the wall and fell headfirst into the ocean. The sputtering device, trailing sparks, splashed into the water beside him. Momentarily, the man surfaced and began flailing in the water.

"Get back in quickly, Joe!" shouted Sue.

"Do the override!" shouted Jo to her crew member who quickly responded.

"Hit reverse!" shouted Sue. Jo had already done that.

"Are you in Joe?" shouted Sue.

"I'm in, and I hit the lock button," he replied.

"OK, wait...wait....Dive, Dive, Dive," Jo shouted, as they continued back while diving, then, she stopped the sub and turned it around.

"Depth?" asked Jo to one of her crew.

"600," the crew replied.

"All ahead full, continue full dive!" Jo shouted as they continued quickly downward and away from the island. Soon, they were heading South again at their previous depth.

"Are they following?" asked Sue.

"Probably, since it's their duty, but these subs are faster than the ships they have at Galapagos, and we should be below the tractor range, so I don't think they'll follow for long. But they'll report the incident."

"However, they don't have aircraft, or satellites," said Sue.

"No, that would be a violation of the ban," said Jo. "They do have super fast chase boats in the Western Pacific, but as far as I know, none of them are down here."

"Then I think we're in the clear," said Sue. "And, so much for a stop."

"Whew....that took quick action, and I would never have thought about how to do it, so you really saved the day, Sue, because I would have nixed it and we'd have been in jail," said Jo. "I think our next stop will be inside the Magellan Strait at the tip of South America."

"Have you ever been there before ?" asked Sue.

"Never," said Jo.

"Then it will be a new adventure for all of us," said Sue.

It would be a little over three days before they reached the southern tip of South America. Even though Jo had never been there, she knew through her training that the Strait of Magellan would be the passage used to cross to the Atlantic Ocean. She pulled up a detailed ocean chart on the screen to locate the Pacific entrance to the Strait, and they entered. They surfaced after they were well into the Strait and began to navigate it on the surface. There had been several small towns on the northern shore as they traveled Eastward, but there was no sign of life in any of them. The one large city, Punta Arenas would be several hours from the Western entrance, and it was nearly that before they rounded a bend and spotted something man-made in the distance. Before they reached what was once the city, they came upon what looked like a long vacant pier made of concrete that was way past needing repairs. After a brief discussion they decided to stop there at the pier because it was almost evening. The structure appeared to be stable enough for them to tie up, and in the relatively calm waters of the Strait it was not difficult for them to dock.

"It looks more like an old highway," said Jo, as her crew secured the sub to what looked like guard rails.

"It is, because you can see it extend out in both directions," said Joe.

"Well, for us it's a dock," said Sue.

It was the beginning of summer in the Southern Hemisphere and the weather had been sunny and relatively mild for this extreme latitude. The road was perfect for everyone to walk on and was a welcome break from living in the confinement of a submarine for so long. Everyone slowly piled out of the sub and walked down the highway to an open area ringed by flowering bushes. It had been six days since anyone had stood on solid earth, so it was a welcome relief for them. As they were wandering about, Sue spotted movement in the distance near some trees.

"It looks like a man, so someone lives here," said Sue.

"He has fine clothes on and has the appearance of being civilized," said Joe.

"Yes, he has very fine clothes, and he's not armed as far as I can tell," said Jo who was now observing him through a small pair of binoculars.

"Well, based on our last stop, I don't think we should take any chances," said Joe who was standing with Sue, Jo, Pat and Cas.

"Do we go to him or wait for him to come to us?" asked Cas.

"Are you kidding, we go to him," said Sue who had already begun walking toward him. Jo went with her, stride for stride. Joe followed, while Cas and Pat remained behind after Joe had held up his hand for them to stay behind.

"Maybe Pat should accompany us with his gun just in case," said Jo.

"Well, maybe it should be Cas since she is less threatening with her pocket pistol," said Joe who turned while he was walking and pointed at Cas, then motioned for her to follow.

"What, for my gun?" asked Cas who soon joined them.

"Yes, I hate it that we have to think like that, but this is too new for us to be casual about anything," said Sue.

"He actually looks quite formal so I'm not sure what that means," said Jo.

"You mean he might have been sent out by someone?" asked Joe.

"I'm not sure, but his clothes look well fitted, his hair is trimmed neatly, and he has a fine jacket on," she replied.

"It is odd to find someone dressed like that out here," said Sue.

"Particularly since I see no sign of a settlement of any kind," said Jo.

"We'll soon see," said Sue, as they approached the man. He remained still, and as they grew near he spoke.

"What brings you here to this godforsaken place," he said, in a distinctly British accent.

"Well, it's a long story," said Sue who stopped a short distance away. Jo, Joe and Cas came to a halt beside her.

"Oh good, you speak English," said the man.

"We do," said Sue.

"I'm Reginald," said the man.

"I'm Sue, this is Jo, Joe and Cas," said Sue.

"So, what does bring you all the way down here to this hell hole?" he replied.

"I guess the short version is that we're escaping what we don't like about the Pacific," said Sue. "And this gorgeous scenery is anything but a hell hole."

"OK, well it is a spectacular natural location, but if you live here by yourself in the winter, you might not find it to your liking," said Reginald.

"You live here by yourself?" asked Sue.

"No, my wife and daughter are up there," he replied, pointing to a large home up on the hill.

"And there are no other people here?" asked Jo.

"Not anywhere," said Reginald.

"That would definitely be lonely," said Sue.

"Well, considering where this is, and after getting a brief but

115

distant look at that crowd of people you came with, you look a bit like asylum seekers," said Reginald.

"No, we're not seeking asylum," said Sue. "We're actually looking for the Emerald City."

"The Emerald City? hmmm….wait….oh, like in the Wizard of Oz?" Reginald asked. "Oh, but this is definitely not the Emerald City."

"But we hope to find it," said Sue.

"Alright, then in your search for the Emerald City, could I join you?….I could be the scarecrow," said Reginald.

"Sure, but I don't think you need a brain," said Sue.

"Oh, I'm not so sure about that," said Reginald.

"And do you dress like this every day?" asked Jo.

"You never know when dignitaries will show up unexpectantly," said Reginald.

"And here we are," said Sue.

"I've continued to have high hopes," said Reginald.

"And look, four hundred of us show up unexpectantly, and here you are, appropriately dressed to meet us," said Sue.

"Four hundred is a migration not a delegation, but I guess that still warrants a formal greeting," said Reginald.

"A migration is probably closer to the truth than you know," said Sue. "A year ago, most of us were primitives living in the wild, eating whatever we could find and pooping in holes." Reginald started to smile as he stared at Sue, then held back a laugh.

"But you conned Jo here into giving you a ride in her sub," he replied.

"That's also very close to the truth," said Sue. "And she's now AWOL among other crimes."

"Where did you start from, California?" he asked.

116

"How did you guess?" asked Sue.

"Who else would have the balls to do what you did and con a sub captain into giving you and a crowd of four hundred a ride with a destination like the Emerald City?" asked Reginald.

"I have to agree with you, Reginald, but I know she doesn't have balls, however I'm really not sure what she does have, but I'll be honest with you, I do want to have what she has," said Jo.

"She's definitely a force from what little I've seen and heard of her," said Reginald.

"Are you familiar with the government policies in the Pacific?" asked Sue.

"Why do you think we're here?" he replied. "My ancestors sailed there from England over three generations ago to escape the Atlantic Basin practices. But they left almost immediately."

"And you're all that's left of those who came here three generations ago?" asked Sue.

"Yes we are, and as you might expect, life here is tough, more like survival," said Reginald. "The three of us have survived alone here now for almost ten years after our elders passed."

"Since your ancestors came from the Atlantic originally, were they religious?" asked Sue.

"Yes, Jewish, and my wife still is," he replied.

"So your ancestors found out that in the Pacific some of those with beliefs might be considered dangerous?" asked Sue.

"Certain beliefs were, and I guess some religions were too," he replied. "But for whatever reason, our ancestors decided to leave," he replied.

"Why did they end up staying here?" asked Sue.

"They didn't like what was going on in the Atlantic side, and after living in the Pacific for awhile and not liking it, where would

117

they go?" he asked.

"Right, neither there nor there," said Jo, pointing one way, then the other.

"I think they would have been much better off to have stayed in the Pacific, but once here we became marooned since our ship was later sunk in a storm while anchored out," said Reginald.

"So, in reality, you had no choice but to stay," said Jo.

"That's true," said Reginald. "And how would we know that not another ship would come through here. None. No ship traffic in the decades since! Total isolation."

"That's a valuable piece of information in and of itself, since we plan to sail into the Atlantic Basin when we leave here," said Jo. "It makes me wonder if there is some reason no ships ever come here."

"I'd be interested to find out," said Reginald. "And you said most of you were recently what? Primitives?" he asked, looking at Sue.

"That's right, not much more than six months ago I was essentially what you would refer to as a savage, or as we referred to ourselves, primitives," said Sue. "Joe had found a time capsule, learned how to read and speak and taught his two kids. He then ended up getting back with his whole tribe, including me. So we learned to read, and I read the dictionary and all books that I could find, cut my hair, took a bath, made some clothes, started pooping and peeing in a makeshift toilet, brushed my teeth, started using Kotex, and suddenly I'm almost civilized." Reginald is now laughing as he came forward to shake her hand and she hugged him.

"Can we come with you, please?" he asked.

"We have no idea where we're going," said Jo.

"Our kind of trip," said Reginald.

118

"Well, from what I've read about this place, if I lived here for one winter, I think I'd try to swim out of here as soon as the weather broke," said Sue.

"I know, this is the beginning of summer, so don't get the idea that it's like this very much of the time," said Reginald.

"Jo, can we fit three more into that tub?" asked Sue.

"Of course," said Jo. "But first, why don't we try to meet your family before it gets dark?"

"Sure, and actually I think my daughter might have followed me down here," he said, turning to scan the bushes before he waved. From behind a tree came a girl who hesitated at first, then walked over to them.

"This is Susan," said Reginald.

"She'll be the third Sue," said Jo. "But as far as I'm concerned there can never be enough Sue's."

"Can you go get your wife?" asked Sue.

"Of course," said Reggie. "I'll go get her and a few things and meet you at the sub. Susan, you go with them."

"What if your wife doesn't want to go?" asked Jo.

"Oh my god, are you kidding, she's wanted to leave here her whole life, so she'll be thrilled to come with you," said Reginald.

"And of course, as we said, we have absolutely no idea where we're going," said Sue.

"Perfect," said Reginald.

"Can we call you Reggie?" asked Sue.

"That's what I was known as when there were other people here," he replied.

"And make it a very few things, no bags, we are traveling as if it's a weekend outing," said Jo.

"No problem," said Reggie.

119

He looked at his daughter and pointed to the sub, then turned and hurried back the way he came. The daughter looked at Sue who smiled and took her hand.

"Susan, I think you'll like the sub," said Sue as they started back toward the sub. "And you'll meet a lot of nice people on the trip."

By the time Reggie and his family had been introduced to everyone, and given a tour of the sub, it was dark. They had already decided to stay the night at the dock so that they would have a daytime view of the Strait on their way out into the Atlantic. Reggie filled them in on what had happened to Punta Arenas, which at one time was the southernmost major city in the world. During the war, the Strait had become a strategic passage for all sides after the Panama Canal had been destroyed, and it too was a casualty of the many battles that ensued. Now it was just rubble as were the other habitable areas in the Strait. So the next morning, as they cruised out of the Strait, there was not much to see except the fabulous scenery. As they headed out into the Atlantic, they were still completely undecided on where to go next, except for the likelihood that they would not be able to stop at any of the major centers, if they still existed. After several lively discussions, they decided to sail to the Caribbean in the hope of finding somewhere that would be safe to visit. Since everyone except Jo and her crew were from America, the rationale was that Americans, even on the Atlantic side, might at least be people they could relate to, despite possible differences in beliefs. They were not at all familiar with the local military capabilities on the Atlantic side, so they had no idea how their submarine might be viewed or dealt with if they came into contact with authorities. As a result, they would travel at depth, and approach any contact with extreme caution. However, Sue felt that perhaps at least someone in the Americas might still be sympathetic to others from the same continent.

Chapter 6

It was five days travel in the submarine from the Strait of Magellan to Puerto Rico, their intended destination. Early in the morning on the sixth day, the sub came to the surface with just the conning tower out of the water. They were stopped in the water off the southeast end of the island near where a US naval base used to be in the far distant past. On shore, there appeared to be someone living in a crudely built structure with what looked like a garage next to it. There were dim lights on in the structure and a figure could be seen moving inside, casting shadows on the white curtains.

"There's too much foul ground to get any closer," said Jo.

"Besides, I don't think your dinghy is a good idea to go to shore in these waves," said Joe.

"I think we'll just wait to see if whoever is in there notices us," said Jo.

"Since we're in unknown waters, maybe we need to make

sure we won't be arrested before we get too brave about meeting anyone," said Sue.

"My thoughts exactly, so my crew is going to be watching the horizon very carefully while we're partially surfaced," said Jo.

"I saw the curtain open a little," said Joe. "And now it looks like the door is opening, so maybe they've spotted us."

"it would be pretty hard to miss this conning tower against the morning sun on the water," said Sue.

"OK, so now someone is outside looking us over," said Jo as she enlarged the image on the screen.

"It's a black woman," said Reggie who had just come into the control center.

"Is that important?" asked Sue.

"I've only heard stories from my ancestors, but I think one of the laws here in the Atlantic has to do with a complete lack of diversity," said Reggie.

"Alright, so how does that translate?" asked Sue.

"Each race or ethnic group has had to be located with their kind," said Reggie.

"So that means total segregation," said Jo.

"That's disgusting, but what we do know, then, is that it is not being enforced by the WO, so it's not considered by them to be something that can lead to another war." said Sue.

"That's true," said Jo. "If it exists here, it is accepted by the WO."

"The other thing we know, is that the WO eliminates certain troublesome tribes from the Pacific. And we suspect that they actually just relocate these tribes to the Atlantic side where they can be segregated with tribes of their belief. Then I assume the Atlantic does what they can to keep them segregated."

"Right, that would be under the purview of the Atlantic Societies," said Jo.

"So then we add beliefs to the segregation categories here in the Atlantic," said Sue.

"Piece by piece, we are learning," said Jo. "But the fact that they require segregation here is not a good thing."

"It's disgusting," said Reggie. "My wife's family was Jewish and they had only a few places they were allowed to live."

"I assume the Gorfs would qualify as a racial group and end up being segregated in some location separate from us," said Sue.

"Assuming there are even any other Neanderthal looking people in the world, and if not, they would be a very small segregated population, isolated from other segregation categories," said Jo.

"If this law segregates Jews, then it must segregate people by religion," said Sue. "I assume Jews fall into the caucasian race. Because what if you're a black Jew? Would you be sent to a black segregation location, or a Jewish segregation location?"

"A black Jew would be mixed religeous? Not a specific race?" asked Reggie.

"That raises the issue of who interprets what is categorized as mixed racial," said Sue. "So, for example, if you had to designate race for segregation purposes, you could make it a maternal priority by law. Then, if the mixed race is black-white with a white mother, the person would be white since the mother is white. But if you made the law a paternal priority, the person would be black if the father was black."

"What if it was a personal choice?" asked Jo.

"That would become totally chaotic," said Sue. "It would have to be something that could be legally enforced. Basing it on racial preference would be clearly racist since the other race would be

123

marginalized in the designation. So making it either maternal or paternal would be the easiest to enforce. And my choice would be maternal since the woman has to carry the baby to term. So if the woman is black, the person is black. And vice versa. Look, the woman does all the work, so she gets the priority."

"Then isn't that racism?" asked Jo.

"Why?" asked Sue.

"By picking white, aren't you marginalizing black?" asked Jo.

"True, but picking black, aren't you marginalizing white, and therefore isn't that also racism?" asked Sue.

"Maybe the term racism is irrelevant in a system that segregates everyone," said Joe.

"It would almost have to be, so maybe you use the term mixed racial," said Jo.

"But if you did that and tried to segregate mixed racial, can you imagine how many different combinations that would entail?" asked Sue. "That would make the entire segregation policy virtually impossible to manage."

"I know, because in the mixed racial category, what if neither parent were either pure white or pure black?" asked Jo.

"Isn't the word pure in reference to race, racist on it's face," asked Sue.

"A rule book is clearly required here," said Jo.

"Look, when we started out, we thought the Atlantic was about belief or non-belief," said Sue. "Then we met Reggie and he said it was segregation. And what is here, if it is segregation, seems to be extraordinarily complex."

"It's impossibly complex," said Reggie. "Because I'm not sure it could be based on religion. Look, there are hundreds of religions, and all of them are not necessarily in love with one another, so if you based it on that, there would be hundreds of segregated places with various religions and races in each."

"Like you said, it's impossibly complex," said Jo.

"As you suggested, we'd need a rule book before we even considered living here," said Sue. "But on the face of it, any form of segregation is a non starter for us. Am I right?"

"You're right," said Jo. "There's no way we're staying here."

"Here, it all depends on who decides what we are and where we go, and then enforces the rules in order to be separated from everyone else who isn't like us," said Sue.

"Why don't we speak with someone who lives here before we over think this any more," said Jo.

"Good idea," said Sue.

"Well, for me, in terms of weather, I think it might be a great place to live," said Reggie. "But in terms of getting along with all of the other things we likely have to live with when we're here, I think I would agree with my ancestors and go somewhere else."

"I know, but the rationale for coming here was the thought that perhaps this was America, and we're American, so we had a chance of being accepted," said Sue.

"Like I said, let's speak with someone who lives here and see what their take is on the matter," said Jo.

"This someone is now walking over to her garage and opening it," said Joe.

"Wait, that looks like some kind of car, not a boat," said Sue.

"I know, you can't drive a car out to us very easily," said Jo.

"It could be a car that floats," said Joe.

"We'll soon find out, because she just got in and it's starting to move out of the garage."

The red and blue vehicle started down the hill on the grass

until it reached the beach and then continued into the ocean, where it bobbed along toward them, crashing through the waves. Jo was now at the controls and the sub began to surface, so that by the time the strange vehicle reached them they were able to go out on deck to greet her. By now Pat had joined them with his pistol after Joe sent for him. Five of them were out on deck. Jo, Sue, Joe, Reggie and Pat.

"Hello," said the woman after she stood up in front of the windshield of the vehicle. She had long curly hair that stood out in all directions.

"Other than hello, do you speak English?" said Sue.

"Of course," said the woman. "I saw the tower of your sub and took a chance that you'd surface and that you would be friendly."

"You don't have government subs here?" asked Sue.

"I have no idea, but we don't get visitors here at all, so anyone or anything that shows up is almost certainly from somewhere else," said the woman.

"So you weren't afraid we were some official coming after you?" asked Sue.

"We've been here a long time and that has never happened," said the woman.

"So it must be pretty safe here," said Sue.

"I don't think anyone knows we're here, because if they did they'd have come after us a long time ago," said the woman.

"Why would they come after you?" asked Sue.

"You're not from anywhere near here are you?" asked the woman.

"We came from California," said Sue.

"California? Oh my god, are you kidding me?" gasped the woman. "Then you have no idea what the rules are for living here

126

do you?"

"Well, only what we've heard, and those are entirely confusing regarding how it would be applied," said Sue.

"What have you heard?" she asked.

"That everyone is segregated and has to live in separate areas," said Sue.

"That's right, and I'm supposed to be in Africa," said the woman. "So do you agree with that policy?"

"Are you kidding, it's entirely absurd," said Sue.

"So why did you come?" she asked.

"Well, first of all we didn't know anything about the rules here when we left," said Sue. "So our logic was that since we're from America we thought those living in the Americas might welcome others from America."

"Well, if it were up to me, I would welcome you with open arms, but the reality is that the authorities here are likely to ship you rather quickly to your segregated area," said the woman.

"Are these authorities able to detect our presence?" asked Jo.

"I assume they can, even in a submarine, so I wouldn't stick around here very long," said the woman.

"What about you?" asked Sue. "Do you like living here on this island?"

"Oh my god, no, I don't like it here and especially what's going on with the authorities here, so I would leave at the very first opportunity," said the woman.

"Well, we've decided to leave the Atlantic entirely as soon as we leave here," said Sue.

"I know it would be way too much for me to ask if I can come with you," said the woman.

"Not at all," said Jo. "We have plenty of room, but is it just you?"

"No, my sister will pee her pants if she finds out we might be able to leave," said the woman.

"OK, well, we don't want your sister to pee all over herself, but we have no idea where we're going," said Sue.

"Fine, as long as its out of here," said the woman.

"We're trying to find somewhere in the world where we can live peacefully without having to conform to someone's distorted version of correct human habitation," said Sue.

"That sounds like paradise to me, but where is that?" asked the woman.

"If we knew we'd be there," said Jo.

"So you don't really know where to look?" asked the woman.

"We have no idea," said Sue. "We're like Dorothy in the Wizard of Oz, looking for the Emerald City."

"Oh my god!.... I absolutely love that!" said the woman. "Look at me, I could be the cowardly Lion."

"You're right, you could be the Lion," said Sue. "But I don't think you're a coward."

"Living here since we were children and not doing anything about it?" she replied. "No, I'm a coward."

"I don't know, driving out to a strange submarine?" asked Sue. "That's pretty brave. By the way, I'm Sue, this is Jo, the sub captain, Joe, Reggie and Pat."

"I'm Suzanne," said the woman.

"Quickly, go get your sister and a few bare essentials and get back here as soon as you can," said Jo. "We need to leave before we're detected."

"I'll be right back," said Suzanne who slid back into her seat and zoomed away.

"Is every woman we meet named Sue?" asked Jo. "I don't care but it could become a bit confusing if there are any more."

Less than a half hour later the two women were safely on board and the sub was beginning to get underway when a large boat could be seen coming around the island and heading toward them. Jo had already secured the doors and was beginning to dive, so she quickly went to full ahead toward deeper water. Above they could hear the drone of the engines in the distance, unsure whether they had tractor beam capability, or something akin to it. Jo continued to dive at a speed that was now outrunning the surface craft. As they went deeper the sound of the engines grew fainter. She stayed deep and as they cleared the last island in the Caribbean, no sound from the pursuing boat could be heard. As they settled into their usual silent running the conversation shifted back to the issue of where they were headed next, and how long it would be until they got there.

"This sub is amazing," said Suzanne, who was in the control center with Jo, Sue, Reggie and Joe.

"It is, but after awhile you'll still want to put your feet on solid ground," said Jo.

"I'm sure, so where are you going next so I can do that?" asked Suzanne.

"We were thinking we'd start at the Cape of South Africa," said Jo. "If there's nothing there or if we don't like it, we would go all the way around and explore the East coast of Africa to see what regulations are in place there."

"Well, if the weather at the Cape is anything like the Horn of South America, I'd be for just continuing around," said Reggie.

"I'm pretty sure it's not," said Sue. "It's at a latitude comparable to Southern California where we used to live, and that was very mild."

"Great," said Reggie.

"How long to get there?" asked Joe.

"I figure it would be about six days, according to the charts," said Sue.

"Yes, about six days, but I'll get a little more accurate reading once I put in the exact coordinates," said Jo.

"So I assume you'll stop at the Cape?" asked Suzanne.

"If we can, yes," said Jo. "It depends on what's there. We want to be among people and not in a deserted area. We have been extremely careful so far in picking where we land since we have no idea whether we'll find friend or foe. We have to proceed with caution."

"We might find that the Cape is not committed to one ocean society or the other, or even if they have any serious regulations at all," said Sue.

"There was literally no one on the Horn of South America," said Jo.

"Except me, my wife and daughter, so I guess we could find a similar situation on the Cape," said Reggie.

"I thought I heard something about the Cape?" said Susie who just walked in.

"Yes, and it's at the same latitude as Southern Cal, only in the southern hemisphere," said Sue.

"So it might have a similar climate?" asked Susie.

"We have no idea, but yes, hopefully," said Sue.

"And if we stop there, it's Africa, so it will be interesting to see how their segregation program is working first hand since that was where I was supposed to reside in joyful separation from all the other segregated people that I wasn't supposed to be in direct contact with," said Suzanne.

"Let's just try to erase segregation from our vocabulary once we leave the Atlantic," said Sue.

"I'm for that," said Suzanne.

Three days later Jo called Sue and Joe to the tower and told them she was hearing the sounds of a large vessel off to Port. This was very unusual since they had not encountered surface vessels of any size out at sea since they left California. Jo said it appeared to be a very large vessel, and was going much slower than they were. Sue suggested they slow up and come closer to the surface so they could get a better idea of what it was, since it didn't make any sense for a military-type vessel to be cruising in the middle of the Atlantic. Jo was still somewhat cautious about that, but slowed and steered to the ship's heading as she slowly rose toward the surface.

"I'm monitoring very carefully for any sign of hostility, and I've heard nothing yet," said Jo.

"I have an idea about what this might be," said Sue. "So can we just go up far enough to have the antennas sticking out so we can put this ship on the screen?"

"Alright, but what are you thinking it might be?" asked Jo.

"When we were in California, there was a large vessel that had gone aground at some time in the distant past there on the beach where you found us," said Sue.

"Do you know what kind of vessel it was?" she asked.

"Well, not exactly, but based on the little bit we were able to uncover, it appeared to be a cruise ship like those that carried thousands of people on vacations to exotic places long ago," said Sue.

"I think I know what you're talking about, but they stopped making them a long time ago," said Jo.

"I know, but perhaps one could still be operational," said Sue. "Or it could have been built by one of the surviving societies since the war.

"Possibly," said Jo.

"They were like a luxury city on the sea," said Sue.

"We had actually uncovered a few spots, and it did seem to be just that," said Joe.

"I've read about them, but we're talking a thousand years or more since they sailed the seas," said Jo. "I'm just not sure if anything like that could still be operational today."

"Like Sue said, maybe one of your surviving societies decided to build them again," said Joe.

"That's true, one of them could have," said Jo. "OK, I'm going up."

"This could be a fascinating find if it is one," said Sue.

"So if it is, do you think it might be where some of the population is actually living full time?" asked Jo.

"Why not?" asked Sue. "It would be a form of segregation. And these ships were very large and apparently had everything one would need to live full time, except food, which they could get at the ports where they stop."

"That would be the issue, considering the segregation policy in the Atlantic," said Jo.

"But in today's world it might not only be possible, but necessary to never have to go ashore at all," said Sue.

"If you could figure out the food issue," said Jo.

"I know, but they would be out here away from the onerous requirements of living in the Atlantic, and they would have an abundance of sea food," said Sue.

"Maybe they could have gardens and grow vegetables," said

Joe.

"I know, why not?" asked Sue.

"We're almost there," said Jo who had called her crew, and a few minutes later they had an antennae above water and had a visual.

Susie and Suzanne, who had become friends, wandered into the control center when they realized the sub was coming to the surface. A moment later, Jack and Reggie came in to see what was going on.

"Interesting," said Jo, now that they had the ship on the screen. "It is exactly what you described, Sue, but it looks new, so clearly it has been manufactured a lot more recently than a thousand years ago."

"Well, that shines a whole new light on who might be in it," said Sue.

"Yes, and I'm not sure it looks like a floating city," said Jo as she studied the image on the screen.

"Where are all the balconies?" asked Susie.

"It does have balconies, but it looks more like it's designed for a lot fewer people than those in the pictures I've seen of cruise ships from the past," said Sue.

"A cruise ship for the rich?" asked Jack.

"It's awfully slick looking compared to those in the history books," said Sue.

"More like a spaceship," said Jo.

"This ship is amazing. It has luxury balconies and who knows what other gizmos I see all over the ship," said Reggie.

"Including quite a bit of plant life," said Joe.

"It almost looks like it just left port," said Jack. "It's so polished."

"Well, this ship does have the appearance of something I'd

133

find in the city I used to live in," said Jo. "It's ultra modern, so it's definitely from an existing city that survived the war with all or most of their technology."

"So how long do you think it's been out here, and who operates it?" asked Jack. "It's in the Atlantic, so is it from a city sympathetic to the regime that promotes segregation, or is it a case where some rich dudes are using it to escape the requirements of segregation?"

"It could definitely be either," said Sue. "It's large and has all of the necessities of city living, so I suspect it could continue to exist out here at least for the lifetimes of those rich dudes, if that's whose on it."

"Can you establish communication with the ship?" asked Jack.

"Wait!" said Sue who had been studying the ship and thinking.

"What?" asked Jo as both she and everyone else waited for Sue to speak.

"There's another possibility here," said Sue who hesitated while still thinking.

"And?" asked Jo.

"I keep thinking about the WO," she replied.

"Well, me too, but what does that have to do with this ship?" asked Jo.

"Where are they?" asked Sue.

"You mean you think they're on this ship?" asked Jo.

"Sure, why not," said Susie. "And maybe other ships, who knows."

"They've been in control for thousands of years, and this ship is relatively recent," said Jo.

"I know, but what I'm thinking is that the WO is, in fact, not a central location but rather a network of individual robots operating collectively from many locations, worldwide," said Sue.

"But think of the computer power needed to process and act upon all of that data," said Jo. "Doesn't that require some kind of mega computer?"

"Times change and technology improves with time," said Sue. "If you think about how this organization was initially formed, and then how it gradually became run by robots, you begin to imagine how that took place, not over night, but in steps that had to include major technological improvements."

"Well, from what I know, they did have a giant computer when it was run by people," said Jo.

"Jo, that was thousands of years ago," said Sue.

"OK, that is a very long time," said Jo. "And you think the computer capabilities have improved quite a bit since then?"

"Hello!" said Sue. "If it didn't, someone was sleeping, and I don't think it was any of the robots."

"OK, you might be on to something," said Jo.

"I think she's right on," said Susie.

"Whether I'm right or wrong, we need to contact them," said Sue.

"I don't know, could they turn out to be hostile toward us?" asked Jo.

"If this is controlled or influenced by WO, which I believe to be true, they've known exactly where we've been and what we've been doing since we left California," said Sue. "And I'm sure they covered our asses at times, maybe all of the time," said Sue.

"I mean, that's possible, yes," said Jo.

"They did," said Sue.

"Yes, but what if they're not WO but an Atlantic authority?" asked Jo.

"Look, I read about deep sea sonar that was here thousands of years ago, so I can't believe that nobody was aware that we traveled over twenty thousand miles undetected," said Sue. "That includes both the Atlantic and Pacific authorities."

"So you're saying that WO has ignored alerts to them from both oceans?" asked Jo.

"We're not invisible, even traveling deep underwater, so yes, absolutely," said Sue.

"So you think I've been kidding myself about not being caught?" asked Jo.

"I think you thought we had been lucky up to now," said Sue.

"You're right about that, because I did know about deep sea sonar," said Jo.

"We had an angel over our shoulder for our whole journey," said Sue.

"And the WO is our angel?" asked Susie.

"Yep," said Sue.

"OK, well, I have an old ship-to-ship radio that ships have used for hundreds of years or more, and I also have a modern one," said Jo.

"Use the modern one," said Sue.

"Sure, here," said Jo who flipped a switch and handed the mic to Sue.

"Cruise ship, this is the submarine you have been escorting from California, traveling beside you a half mile out to your Starboard," said Sue into the mic.

"Ahoy Sue," came a woman's voice over the speaker. "We wondered when you would show up."

"Well, you never let us know where you were," said Sue.

"But you knew we followed you?" asked the woman.

"Of course, how far do you think we would have gotten if you weren't there to protect us?" asked Sue.

"So you already know that we knew you in California from the very beginning," said the woman.

"I didn't know, but I suspected it once I figured out that there had to be something like a WO with the world the way it was," said Sue.

"Jo was AWOL the minute she left from California with your tribe, and they reported it to us," said the woman.

"Of course, and you let us go," said Sue.

"You almost got yourself in trouble in Galapogos, but Joe turned out to be a crack shot," said the woman.

"He is, but I thought guns were illegal in the first place," said Sue.

"They are, except we're the ones who left those guns for you in that time capsule that Joe found."

"Of course, that should have been obvious to me once I figured out that you had to exist," said Sue.

"So we only gave you a few bullets for each gun," said the woman.

"Just enough to allow our tribe to get on it's feet," said Sue.

"Exactly," said the woman.

"And just why did you do that?" asked Sue.

"You were among the survivors living as primitives in what is still the wilderness, and we wanted to see if you could become educated on your own," said the woman.

"You could have done that more directly," said Sue.

"No, we were restricted from directly helping survivors," said the woman. "By directive, each surviving entity must be left to their own abilities, unless it involves activities that might contribute to another big war," said the woman.

"But you helped us travel to here," said Sue.

"No, we just ignored efforts to catch you, which was not direct help," said the woman.

"Are there other wilderness survivors that you've left time capsules for?" asked Sue.

"Worldwide, there are many," said the woman.

"That's kind of what I thought," said Sue. "By the way what's your name?"

"Ellen 554" said the woman.

"I'll call you Ellen if I may," said Sue. "I like you, Ellen, not as a robot, but as a person."

"Thank you, Sue, I like you too, not as a robot but as a person" said Ellen.

"Would it break all of your rules if you were to travel with us on our journey, Ellen," said Sue.

"Only if you let me be the Tin Man," said Ellen.

"Well, you definitely don't need a heart, but you might qualify as a result of your composition," said Sue. "So, yes, you are now the Tin Man, or let's modify that and call you the Tin Woman."

"I accept the invitation and the modification," said Ellen.

"When can you join us?" asked Sue.

"Let me make some arrangements here and then I'll come out to you in a launch," said Ellen.

"We'll be looking for you," said Sue.

"I'll surface," said Jo, as the sub began to rise to the surface. Sue was first to go out onto the deck. Before long, Reggie, Susie, Jack, Joe and Suzanne were out there with her. The cruise ship slowed down and Jo slowed the sub to match their speed. Soon, a launch was lowered into the water and it was not long before it was heading toward them. They welcomed Ellen as she arrived and she sent the launch back to the cruise ship.

"Welcome," said Sue who was right there to hug Ellen.

"Thank you, and oh my god, I've never hugged a human before," said Ellen.

"You might have to get used to it," said Susie as she and the others came forward to hug her.

"Ellen, you look and feel just like one of us," said Sue. "So don't be surprised if we begin to treat you like one of us humans,"

"I look forward to it," said Ellen. "We have a ship of mostly robots and we do have programming that directs us to perform our duties, but we also have the capability to behave like humans, and blend in with humans if we need to."

"That's truly amazing," said Sue. "You are amazing. So do you live forever, or do you wear out at some point?

"No human has ever asked that question of me," said Ellen. "I can answer that since the programmers apparently never thought anyone would ask."

"Sue asks anything, and literally says anything she wants to, so you might have to get used to her," said Jo who had just joined them on deck.

"You're Jo, the captain," said Ellen. Jo nodded.

"To answer your question, Sue, no, we do not live forever," said Ellen. "We have a half life of about fifty years, then we are rehabbed and updated and essentially become another robot. So my lifespan is only fifty years, then my body becomes someone else."

"Oh, I'm sorry for you, but is there a reason for that?" asked Sue.

"It's a safeguard against the possibility of robots becoming more like a human and then changing from our primary directives," said Jo.

"So it's a self regulating robot society, if you will," said Sue.

"You are correct," said Ellen.

"And how old are you now?" asked Sue.

"I'm 35," said Ellen.

"You said you're programmed to interface with, and essentially become, for all intents and purposes, a human," said Sue.

"Not become a human, but pass as a human," said Ellen.

"Right, so this suggests that the WO, as an interactive, cooperative organization of millions, that could theoretically be located everywhere, rather than concentrated in specific locations," said Sue.

"You are correct again," said Ellen. "I'm impressed."

"I'm just saying what seems to actually make sense," said Sue.

"I know, but not many humans understand things the way you do," said Ellen.

"OK, and I'm one of those humans that doesn't quite understand, so clue me in, Sue," said Jo.

"Sure, the WO is made up of most likely millions of robots like Ellen, distributed throughout the entire planet, living among the human population," said Sue. "Each robot has a unique appearance, like humans. Different WO robots have different specialties. I'm not sure how many specialties they have, but the distribution of specialties takes into account the distribution of necessary skills that are needed around the world. As a result they are able to attend to any human requirement, anywhere."

"She's right," said Ellen. "I'm outed. The WO is outed."

"So my next question is: if your primary mission is to prevent another major war, why is your hardware, vis a vis, your robots, designed to help the remaining humans survive?" asked Sue.

"The answer to that is both simple and logical: why should we prevent another war if there are no humans left to protect?" asked Ellen.

"Very good, Ellen," said Sue. "See, I'm not as smart as you thought."

"But you already knew that," said Ellen.

"I assumed it, but I wanted you to say it," said Sue.

"Because otherwise we, meaning the WO, would simply have taken over the world and wouldn't give a shit about the humans."

"You took the words right out of my mouth," said Sue.

"I know, but you do use that word a lot," said Ellen.

"So then, I also suspect that you are deliberately farming humans like us, if I might use the term farming," said Sue. "You gave us primitives basic knowledge, without bias, making sure our initial education is free of beliefs and ideologies, so that we mature without preconceived ideas about how we should live our lives."

"OK, yes, farming is a bit harsh even though it in fact describes quite well what we are doing," said Ellen.

"For the record, I don't mind being farmed because I understand what it means for world peace," said Sue. "However, our little tribe will be such a tiny speck among the world population, will we not?"

"Oh, not at all," said Ellen. "You have no idea how much wilderness exists out there, and how many other tribes are being farmed."

"You're right, I don't, so I stand corrected," said Sue. "And now I understand and appreciate how firmly you have had to deal with counter measures being promoted by those who wish to spread their beliefs to everyone they can. I think they see what you're doing as dictatorial and contrary to their mission, which they believe everyone should have."

"I'm sure they do," said Ellen. "But then, there's a fine line between beliefs that are peaceful and founded in love, and those that are potentially disruptive and dangerous despite their stated intent."

"Let me speculate again," said Sue.

"I think I know what you're thinking, but go ahead," said Ellen.

"OK, so in a world that has a WO to make sure that wars are a thing of the past, and more likely than not, also with robots and mechanization that has removed the incentive to become educated…. many if not most of the population has become essentially lazy, since the need to study and become more knowledgeable has literally disappeared. So the WO is farming primitives who are like children and open to the wonder of knowledge. Therefore keeping the human race from deteriorating into a drunken party on the beach."

"You have described what we're doing perfectly, Sue," said Ellen.

"I'm only speaking for myself, but welcome aboard, Ellen," said Sue. "You can be my farmer anytime you want."

"Mine too," said Susie.

"I think without any doubt that this entire sub full of former primitives will feel quite comfortable to have you join us," said Jo. "And I hope your stay will be permanent."

"It is, because by joining you, this became my assignment, and Sue just made my job so much easier by explaining it to everyone," said Ellen.

"I hope you didn't mind this entire conversation being broadcast ship-wide," said Jo. "As a result, you're likely to now have an entire ship full of fans," said Jo.

"I knew it was shipwide since your monitor here had my face in it," said Ellen. "I think this will be the start of a wonderful relationship. Now, your plan appears to be taking you to the Cape of South Africa."

"Yes," said Jo.

"Were you planning to stop there?" asked Ellen.

"If we can, yes," said Jo.

"Good, so could I be given a duty to perform as a passenger?" asked Ellen.

"Sure, so what are your programmed skills that would be beneficial to humans?" asked Sue.

"My programming includes medical doctor, dentist, and just about every medical skill necessary to repair and keep humans alive," said Ellen.

"Well, we definitely need all of those skills since we currently have none of them," said Sue.

"As your farmer, I guess I knew that," said Ellen "Now, I assume you wanted to stop at the Cape if you could find a friendly population?"

"Ideally, yes," said Jo.

"There is a facility there with a population that has not committed any banned offenses," said Ellen. "So I think it might be a good place to stop to see what you find."

"What she says," said Sue who looked at Ellen and smiled with a slight nod.

"We'll look for it when we get to the Cape," said Jo.

It would be several days before they approached the Cape of Good Hope. Ellen had become just one of the tribe as she was able to meet and chat with a number of them. They rounded the Cape and by the early evening they spotted a greenish glow ahead that lit up the horizon and sent a greenish reflection out into the ocean. As they grew nearer, it became obvious that whatever this was, it was very big. It was as if they were approaching a major city. The closer they came, the brighter and brighter the glow became, and, upon entering the bay they came upon a mega structure that took up the entire screen. It was over a mile wide, with thousands of windows spewing its greenish light into the sky and out onto the water. The sky was aglow from the brightness as Jo brought the sub to a stop a quarter of a mile from a large arched entrance at the structure's base. Above the arch was a neon sign with all but two of it's letters out. The two letters that remained were O and Z. Sue looked at Jo, then back at Ellen who stood behind them.

"I had nothing to do with that," said Ellen with a shrug.

"Then is this just a coincidence, or is it something else?" asked Jo.

"I don't know, but I'm beginning to feel it," said Sue.

The huge entrance began at the water line, suggesting that a ship could pass into the structure. Jo brought the sub to the surface and they waited for someone or something to notice them. But after awhile, Jo began moving the sub slowly forward toward the opening. But the seas were fairly high, and the waves crashed against the structure on either side of the entrance, sending spray into the air. Jo stopped the sub and waited. When they did not receive a reply on the modern radio, she hailed them again on an old fashioned radio she had on the sub for communicating with older craft. The six of them, Jo, Sue, Joe, Ellen and two of her crew, waited patiently, contemplating what to do next.

"I don't see a soul anywhere," said Joe. "I would think that someone inside would appear in one of the thousands of windows, but I don't see anyone."

"Well, it's lit up as if it's a vibrant city, so there has to be someone inside," said Jo.

"It couldn't be totally empty, it's such an elegant city with all of those lights," said Sue. "And you already called them on two different radios, so either their radios are inactive or there is no one monitoring calls."

"I'm not sure what their surveillance system is, but I do have another, really old fashioned, signaling system," said Jo.

"You do, a loudspeaker," said Ellen.

"Right," said Jo.

"Well, South Africa used to be English speaking in the distant past, so one would assume they will be able to understand whatever we say on a loudspeaker," said Sue.

"OK, Sue, you're on," said Jo, handing Sue the mic who took it with an ear to ear grin.

"Hello, Emerald City!" said Sue into the mic. They waited.

"We're aware of you, submarine, what is your business?" came the booming reply in a heavy British accent.

"We're from California looking for the Wizard of OZ and we assume that this is the Emerald City," said Sue, looking at Jo, smiling and then shrugging.

"The Emerald?....Wait!... California?... No way!" came the reply.

"Way!" Sue replied.

"Well, don't just sit there Dorothy, come on in," came the reply. "I'll open the baffles and turn on the lights in our reception bay and you can dock inside." Two large baffles in the entrance swung open and lights came on inside the tunnel as they started in. Green arrows appeared on the side walls as they entered. The baffles, that blocked the ocean waves from entering the structure, swung shut behind them. After a short trip, they pulled up to a dock where three men stood waiting. One black, one brown and the other white. They helped Jo's crew secure the sub to the dock, and the tribe began pouring out of the sub and onto a wide and long dock area.

"We hailed you on the radio, but nobody answered," said Jo with a shrug as she went up to the three men.

"Our radios have been dead for years," said one of them.

"But you heard us on speaker," said Jo.

"We do pick up sounds inside if they're right outside of this entry," he replied.

"We were, yes," said Jo.

"The person who answered us had a British accent," said Sue.

"That would be Colin upstairs, he's the CEO of this complex," said the man.

"How many of you are there in the sub?" asked the man as people kept pouring out and filling the enormous landing.

"Somewhere in the vicinity of four hundred," said Jo.

"Four hundred?" asked the man in a surprised tone.

"At least four hundred," said Sue. "Most of us are educated primitives from California and Jo and her crew were nice enough to help us escape in her submarine."

"Primitives?…escape?…escape from what?….what are you talking about?" the man sputtered.

"It's a long story, but yes, primitives, even though we almost look like normal people, and many of us speak English," said Sue.

"What do you mean, like real people...uh….I'd like to call Colin if you don't mind," said the man, looking entirely confused.

"Better yet, we'd like to just speak with him ourselves in person if we can," said Sue.

"Um, alright, I'll see if he'll agree to that," said the man. He went into a little room and spoke on a device, then returned a moment later.

"He said to just bring whomever is in charge upstairs," said the man.

"That's fine," said Sue, looking at Jo who shrugged and pointed at her.

"OK, but I think both you and the captain of your submarine should come with me," said the man pointing to a hallway.

"Sure thing, but can my assistant Ellen come too?" asked Sue who looked at Ellen who nodded with a smile.

"OK but just the three of you," said the man.

They followed him down the hall to an elevator, and were soon in an upper level with a wall of windows on the ocean side. Exotic modern furniture and fixtures were everywhere, and the bright, slightly green light, made it seem as if they were in full sunlight. A moment later a tall man with a cleanly shaven face and wearing a neatly tailored suit walked in.

"I'm Colin, the director here," he said holding out his hand.

"I'm Jo, captain of that sub and this is Sue, leader of her people, and her assistant, Ellen," said Jo.

"I overheard some of that from below," said Colin. "What's this about primitives?"

"I'll give you the brief explanation," said Sue.

"I'm listening," said Colin.

"OK, so many survivors from the big war escaped the devastation by retreating into the wilderness to live off the land." Sue began. "That was especially true in America, which I understand was pretty much turned into ashes. Then, over the

147

centuries, without the resources and outside contacts of civilized society, they regressed into nothing short of our primitive ancestors of fifty thousand years ago. But then, about twenty years ago one of those from our tribe found a time capsule and a vault. He used the materials and equipment inside to learn how to read, and eventually how to speak. With supplies found in a sealed vault, including a library of books and other useful items, he and his woman became educated primitives, if you will. They had two children, and they taught them what they had learned. Years later, his two children returned to their tribe, only to find it had been besieged by another tribe. They brought those who remained back to where their father had found the time capsule and taught them how to read and everything else. I'm one of those he brought back. So I'm basically an educated primitive, and almost everyone in the sub below has a similar story. We have become somewhat civilized, and may look like civilized people, but we are all just educated primitives. One group that is now in our tribe had somehow evolved into a slightly different physical shape than us, similar in appearance to the Neanderthals, but they are in every way the same, just educated primitives like myself."

"Wow, now that's some story young lady," said Colin. "And by the way, I'd like to hire you as my assistant."

"Her tribe and her man would never let you do that, and neither would I since she's become my mentor, and in every way, our leader," said Jo.

"I'm sure you wouldn't, but we have a severe shortage of educated people here," said Colin.

"Which is not inconsistent with most of the civilized world, Colin," said Ellen.

"I sort of assumed that, but didn't really know," said Colin.

"This complex was built centuries ago by survivors who at the time had all of the intelligence, skills and resources to create this incredible complex. But the skills and intelligence slowly faded over time and the hunger for knowledge among the population has all but disappeared. I preside over lazy, intellectually dumb people who simply expect to have all of their needs taken care of. There are a few, like this man here and the two below, that help me keep this facility from becoming a slowly dying vacation paradise for those who live here."

"I think we might be able to help you, Colin," said Sue. "Our quest, if you can call it that, is to find somewhere that is not under siege by those who have established governments with entirely unacceptable rules for living, and then establish a world class place of learning for those who live here."

"Well, I know about the segregationists in the Atlantic, and since I'm mixed racial, I entirely reject that set of rules like you do," said Colin. "I can assure you that this place is free of those types of controls."

"I'm pleased to hear that," said Sue. "We characterized our quest for a suitable place to live as a search for the Emerald City like in the Wizard of Oz, which was one of the books in the library that our people found," said Sue.

"I can't think of anything more appropriate, considering the state of affairs today in the world," said Colin, nodding. "And look, we have a bit of green in this building, so maybe this is in fact the Emerald City, but I wouldn't call myself the Wizard of Oz by any measure. However, I'm sure we have none of the nonsense about segregation and whatever other unacceptable rules you were under back in California."

"Actually, we left there because we didn't understand what was happening," said Sue. "We only recently found out that what was happening was being managed by the World Organization, and its purpose was to prevent certain types of beliefs from taking root," said Sue. The WO also were the ones who planted our time capsule and the startup materials that have allowed us to become what you see today in our people. Their purpose was to allow primitives to become educated without the biases and beliefs of the past in an effort to begin integrating them into a society that has declined in the desire for greater intelligence over the centuries."

"We made it appear to be thousands of years ago, but the time capsules we placed were put there relatively recently with materials that are from long ago," said Ellen.

"Thank you for that Ellen, that clears up an inconsistency for me," said Sue. "I had trouble rectifying Roy Rodgers with ultra modern WO tech."

"So, Sue, your entire existence, and the existence of your tribe, is a product of the WO and their oversight?" asked Colin.

"Yes," said Sue. "We refer to what they did, and are doing, as farming humans to become potentially more peaceful people."

"And then this farming is worldwide?" asked Colin.

"Yes," said Ellen.

"Ellen, you register on our scan as a robot, so I assume you are a WO robot?" asked Colin.

"That would be correct," said Ellen.

"And right now she's acting as my assistant," said Sue.

"Oh, OK, but in what way?" asked Colin.

"Since they created us, it is now important for them to help guide us in their mission to improve the intelligence of the world," said Sue. "And since they cannot become directly involved in that, they can only act as advisors. So she's my advisor because I and my tribe are the ones who will have to carry this out."

"I see, and if that's not an assistant, I don't know what is," said Colin.

"On that note, welcome to the Emerald City, Ellen. I know about the WO and I consider them my guardian, so forgive me if I worship you."

"Thank you, Colin, but I'm just a robot, not a god," said Ellen. "I joined them recently from a cruise ship that I was on. I volunteered to be the Tin Man on their mission, and was accepted in the search for the Emerald City. And here we are."

"This whole thing is like a dream," said Colin.

"It is definitely like a dream for us too, Colin, so would we be welcome to stay here for awhile?" asked Sue.

"Oh my god, yes, please," said Colin. "And make your stay permanent if you can."

"I can't promise anything since I haven't yet spoken with members of our tribe, but right now this seems very promising," said Sue.

"Well, this complex has no oppressive rules, but it is no Nirvana either, because Nirvana doesn't exist anywhere, but it is a very large, comfortable and friendly place to live," said Colin.

"There are over four hundred of us, so hopefully that will not stress the capacity of your place," said Jo.

"This complex, this compact city if you will, was designed to house twenty five thousand, and we now have fewer than a thousand living here, so space is not a problem," he replied.

"Yes, but what about food?" asked Sue.

"We'll need help with that, but we live on the ocean, so we have access to a good source of protein, and there are gardens nearby that can produce a lot more than they have in the past," said Colin.

"We're certainly willing to put in whatever effort necessary to make things work," said Sue.

"The truth is, we are at a critical point in our life here in this complex," said Colin. "Our very existence depends on our ability to survive on our own, and as I said before, we are beginning to fail in that endeavor. In speaking with you, I detect a unique ability to make things work. It's an ability to create the conditions necessary to survive wherever you are planted. We don't have a lot of that here. So I believe that you and your people will be able to save this complex from eventual abandonment."

"We obviously cannot make any promises, but from what I know about our people, and about the mission of the WO, I know we will work as hard as it takes to make this a viable home for everyone," said Sue. "As I listen to your description of your complex. I can begin to understand what is happening here, as well as elsewhere in the world. But from what I have learned so far as a civilized human, I am convinced that the key to the survival of our civilization is education. Primitives can survive in the wild, but in order to reach the level of achievement that it took to create this complex, we must educate ourselves, and keep educating ourselves."

"I know, and that education must eventually include the technical skills necessary to create what you see here," said Colin.

"Look, what I'm talking about is turning the Emerald City into a place of learning that will produce doctors, engineers and other skills that are needed to not just maintain this style of living, but make it grow," said Sue.

"You mean you want to turn the Emerald City into a college?" asked Colin.

"Forget the old terms, I'm thinking about it becoming a place of learning that is a fun part of everyone's daily life," said Sue. "We have a small library of books and I'm sure this complex has an extensive store of books and other forms of knowledge that is more than sufficient to teach people what we need to know in order to keep, and then greatly expand its function, as well as the function of the surrounding area."

"And the world," said Ellen.

"Do you think you have the people who can do that?" asked Colin.

"I believe that virtually any human can do that if they try," said Sue. "Of course some will be more motivated and better able to operate independently than others," said Sue. "Those individuals will take the lead in their field of knowledge and share it with others."

"You're making me feel that what you propose is actually possible," said Colin.

"Of course it is," said Sue. "Anything is possible if you believe in it, and are willing to spend the time to reach it."

"People like you are rare," said Colin.

"No, the sub is full of people like me who are ready and willing to live here and begin to turn this magnificent city into a place of learning," said Sue.

"Not only that, but this city can be a model for other cities of the world where we are assisting in the education of former primitives," said Ellen.

"Alright then, let's get going," said Colin. "And you know what Sue? If this is the Emerald City, I believe you are in fact the Wizard of Oz."

www.ingramcontent.com/pod-product-compliance
Lightning Source LLC
Chambersburg PA
CBHW030346180626
46812CB00007B/2777